# STOP ME

# STOP ME

RICHARD JAY PARKER

First published in Great Britain in 2009 by
Allison & Busby Limited
13 Charlotte Mews
London W1T 4EJ
*www.allisonandbusby.com*

A CIP catalogue record for this book is available from
the British Library.

10 9 8 7 6 5 4 3 2 1

13-ISBN 978-0-7490-0707-2

Typeset in 11/18 pt Century Schoolbook by
Allison & Busby Ltd

Paper used in this publication is from sustainably managed sources.
All of the wood used is procured from legal sources and is fully traceable.
The producing mill uses schemes such as ISO 14001
to monitor environmental impact.

Printed and bound in the UK by
CPI Mackays, Chatham ME5 8TD

RICHARD JAY PARKER was born in South Wales but moved to London where he enjoyed a successful career as a TV scriptwriter, script editor and producer. He now lives in Salisbury.

www.richardjayparker.com

*To Anne-Marie –*
*for love, smiles and support...and for waiting.*

# Chapter 1

On Monday, February 5th 2007 johnnya@apex.com received an email.

*howdy doody,*

*on vacation*

*slim, attractive dreadlocked babe with a fun sticky-out bellybutton, likes rabbit fur*

*forward this email to ten friends*

*each of those friends must forward it to ten friends*

*maybe one of those friends of friends of friends will be one of my friends*

*if this email ends up in my inbox within a week I wont slit the bitchs throat*

*can you afford not to send this on to ten friends?*

*vk*

On Tuesday, February 6th 2007 johnnya@apex.com deleted the email without reading it.

johnnyb did the same; johnnyc's girlfriend opened their shared inbox, read the email and was troubled by it. She discussed it with her boyfriend when he came home from softball and he told her to delete it.

johnnyd was thirteen. He added the following:

*am forwarding this because it freaks me out. If you want the bitch to die don't forward!!!!!!!!!*

Of remaining johnnies e-z, only sixteen people read the email. johnnyt showed it to his wife. It alarmed them both. They decided it was a sick hoax but forwarded it anyway. They added:

*Sorry about this, folks. This is obviously a practical joke but passing it on. Make your own decision. John and Pat*

They went to bed but couldn't sleep because of it. johnnyt's wife was furious with him. She'd been against the idea of going online in the first place. Did two people in their eighties really need to have a computer if that's the sort of thing it brought into their home?

Of the remaining fifteen random johnnies the email was sent to, only one more person didn't immediately delete it. johnnyv probably wouldn't have forwarded it but his daughter, who unknown to him was up-to-speed with his iPhone, had opened his emails and sent the message to everyone in his address book.

However, despite the rapid proliferation of the email from its starting point of johnnies d, t and v, on Tuesday, February 13th 2007 a package with a local postmark arrived at the Wyoming Police Department. It contained a bedraggled rabbit skin scarf. Wrapped in it was the boiled jawbone of Cody Solomon.

Even though it had arrived in thirty-eight thousand inboxes worldwide, police in the vicinity were completely unaware of the email. Cody Solomon was an itinerant prostitute with dreadlocks and an inverted navel.

On Monday, November 12th 2007, leosharpe@ techflex.co.uk found an email in his work inbox. It had already been forwarded hundreds of times and had reached him because he was in the address book of a small travel insurance company he'd emailed fourteen months previously.

*howdy doody,*

*on vacation in the uk*

*slim, attractive brunette with capped teeth*

*forward this email to ten friends*

*each of those friends must forward it to ten friends*

*maybe one of those friends of friends of friends will be one of my friends*

*if this email ends up in my inbox within a week I wont slit the bitchs throat*

*can you afford not to send this on to ten friends?*

*vk*

Leo had heard about the other emails that had been sent. It had been all over the TV news. He knew that vk stood for Vacation Killer and that seven women had been murdered in the US, two in Germany and one in the UK. The story had gradually become more prominent and then front page when it appeared vk had targeted the British Isles. Teresa Strickland had been his first British victim. A customary block email had been circulated ten days before her jawbone had been sent to Wandsworth police station.

He did consider forwarding the email, but instead picked up the phone and reported it to IT. As the hysteria about vk had risen, so had the amount of hoax emails. They told him to delete it.

Ten days later, Vicky Cordingley's jawbone was sent to Southwark police station. It had capped teeth.

A month later Leo was still troubled by his failure to forward the email but tried to put it from his mind as he prepared to tell Laura about the surprise trip he'd arranged as a Christmas present. The Lake District was Laura's favourite destination and Leo had soon adopted it as his. They both enjoyed being alone together and didn't seek the company of others like so many of their friends did. They could lose themselves in its remoteness and not see another soul for days.

A waitress deposited a plate of appetisers on the low table in front of their usual sofa in Chevalier's Bar and Laura thanked her before dumping her coat on the arm and making her way to the ladies. He anticipated her reaction when she got back, her smile wrinkling the band of freckles across the bridge of her nose and puffing her henna curls from her face to kiss him.

He felt excitement expanding in his chest. He was useless at keeping secrets and marvelled at how he'd managed to keep his mouth shut. They'd both taken the afternoon off for Christmas shopping and the plan was to have a boozy lunch and then go home for a cosy dinner in the evening. After she'd left the house for work that morning he'd also decked out the rooms with a secret stash of decorations he'd been stockpiling – it would all be waiting for her when they got back. Leo nibbled an olive off a stone and, having decided how he would break the news, settled back and waited for Laura to return from the ladies.

At first Leo thought she might have been chatting to Hektor. He was the fifty-something owner of Chevalier's and Greek sugar daddy to a procession of female staff members. His effortless, Mediterranean good looks normally resided nonchalantly between the kitchen and bar. So it was over ten minutes before Leo rose from the sofa and went to find Laura, first checking the different levels of the bar and then tentatively poking his head round the door of the ladies. There was no sign of her.

Laura worked on the first floor of the Opallios office block behind Chevalier's but he knew she wouldn't be there. He knew before he left the bar by the back entrance, crossed the street and buzzed the intercom to be let in. The rain re-invigorated itself while he waited and pinged off the grill while an incoherent voice asked him to identify himself.

'Leo Sharpe...Laura's husband.'

His feeling of dread mounted as he climbed the stairwell, but he had his anger to keep it in check – did Laura not realise how her wandering off would worry him?

When he got to the first floor Maggie Allan-Carlin, Laura's boss, was there to meet him. He vaguely recalled being introduced to her at an office party some months before.

Laura had worked at Opallios for over two years. The small but prominent company dealt in international metals and minerals markets and Laura was a promising trainee analyst under Maggie, who was co-director and married to its founder, Joe. Maggie was elegant in an angular way, deeply tanned and fifty-something. Her dyed black hair was always drawn back severely from her face and tied in a bun.

'Leo?' Her dry throat rasped his name and let it hang in the air as if to test its relevance to the pristine atmosphere in the office.

'Is Laura here?' But as he watched a frown attempting to crease her Botox work he immediately regretted wasting his time.

'Wasn't she meeting you to go Christmas shopping?'

Leo nodded silently. Maggie began to say something else but he didn't hear as he was already halfway down the stairs.

He felt prickling spines of unease piercing the tops of his shoulders when he re-entered the bar. He checked the ladies for a second time and didn't register the protests of the two occupants. Neither of them was Laura. He briefly caught his own reflection in the vast mirror – rain had plastered the hair to his face and panic was soaking through his features. The man who stared back at him was a complete stranger to the shaved, twenty-nine-year-old face he'd been greeted by over the sink that morning.

It was then he realised the un-Laura like behaviour was not her own choice.

He sat back down on the couch and stared at the barely touched dish of olives. He told himself he wouldn't be angry with her if she came back. A couple hovered, waiting for him to vacate his seat and eventually he snapped at them, telling them he was waiting for somebody. They left but the bar was busy and as other smaller groups of people took their place, they eyed the seats too.

Where had she headed when she'd left him? Leo had no more registered her progress to the ladies as he would have if they'd been at home. The bar was long and narrow but split into three levels. The toilets were on the middle level. She could have turned into them or carried on into the other bar. Whatever she'd done – even if he tried to watch her from where he sat – she would have been out of sight.

A waitress tried to take away the dish.

'Can you leave that, please?' He looked at her waist.

'Are you going to order anything else?' she replied in the same blunt manner he'd used.

He got up a few moments later and, as he left, turned to see people sitting in the seats and the plates being removed.

He left Chevalier's by the back entrance again, crossed the street and buzzed to be let into Opallios. Over an hour had passed since they'd sat together on the sofa. Laura had said she was popping to the ladies two minutes after she'd arrived. Leo climbed the stairwell again concocting unlikely scenarios that meant she'd returned to the office and would be sitting back at her desk.

'Still not found her?' Maggie's expression had softened and genuine concern registered.

Leo swallowed and shook his head helplessly.

'I'm sure she'll turn up.' She didn't sound convinced. 'Let's see if her car's still here.'

She took him down the back staircase to the staff car park to see if Laura's Peugeot was still there. It was.

# CHAPTER 2

After Laura disappeared the police watched Leo's house. Even though he'd filed the missing report a couple of hours after she'd vanished he knew he'd automatically be the prime suspect.

He'd been staggered by the sluggishness of the process. He'd had to wait twenty-four hours before his report could be made official, and the first house search hadn't been made until three days later. As soon as his description of her had been tied to an email that had been circulating, however, a step up in manpower was immediately noticeable.

*howdy doody,*

*still in the uk*

*tall, freckle faced, chicken pox scar on left eyebrow*

*forward this email to ten friends*

*each of those friends must forward it to ten friends*

*maybe one of those friends of friends of friends will be one of my friends*

*if this email ends up in my inbox within a week I wont slit the bitchs throat*

*can you afford not to send this on to ten friends?*

*vk*

Leo first saw the email when an investigating officer thrust a copy under his nose. It was circulated three days after she vanished and by that time the authorities were keeping tabs on every similar email being sent. There were thousands of them. Bored office workers with nothing better to do. But this was the only one to describe Laura. The chicken pox scar was one of the distinguishing features Leo had mentioned when he'd reported her missing.

Every day, every minute he anticipated the call. He knew what had happened to Teresa Strickland and Vicky Cordingley as well as the Vacation Killer's seven US victims and two German victims; knew what was meant to come next. But the gap between the email and the parcel turning up widened and although this raised Leo's hopes that she was still alive it also meant that the police suspected him even more.

There were countless investigating officers he had to talk to at his home and at the station and it was when he realised that a surveillance vehicle was following him to work that the emotions that he'd been keeping in check fragmented.

Laura's face was on every paper, news site and TV screen and wherever he went it felt like somebody was always standing outside, trying to see through the wall. He felt paralysed and vulnerable, his life taken effortlessly out of his hands. He asked his interrogators about the car following him and their responses ranged from flat denial to reassurances that it was there for his own benefit.

This intensely floodlit period was barely thirteen days but it felt like the longest two weeks of his existence and he felt ashamed to find himself hoping that that the Vacation Killer would kill again so the focus could shift away from him and Laura. The implications when it did happen, however, robbed him of any time for relief.

Maggie and Jo Allan-Carlin publicly offered a £50,000 reward for information leading to Laura's whereabouts – an unstinting gesture funded by Opallios. Two weeks later their son, Louis Allan-Carlin, disappeared. His boiled jawbone was posted to the police ten days after.

If they hadn't offered the reward money for Laura it seemed quite possible their son would still be alive. At least, that's how Leo would have seen it. The Allan-Carlins never saw the email that circulated a week before Louis made his last visit to them.

*howdy doody,*

*still in the uk*

*good looking, true blonde, 50 or more?*

*forward this email to ten friends*

*each of those friends must forward it to ten friends*

*maybe one of those friends of friends of friends will be one of my friends*

*if this email ends up in my inbox within a week I wont slit the bitchs throat*

*can you afford not to send this on to ten friends?*

*vk*

The dispersal of the emails the Vacation Killer sent varied. Sometimes it appeared as if the victim were being watched and in others that they'd already been captured. It made no difference, the Vacation Killer always made good on the promise.

Louis Allan-Carlin was the true blonde in question and Leo was convinced the number in the email referred to the £50,000 reward money.

The Allan-Carlins had become reluctant participants. A media that quickly counter-speculated that her disappearance and the description in the email were a coincidence – or that the email itself was a hoax – quickly dismissed Laura. There were thousands of such emails circulating by then and his interrogators insinuated that it was an opportunist way of misdirecting police towards a high-profile murder enquiry.

Had the Vacation Killer wearied of the investigation taking a wrong turn and murdered Louis Allan-Carlin to turn the spotlight back on track? When a parcel containing his jawbone had been sent to the police and there was still no trace of Laura, the investigation into her disappearance was stepped down. But was their investigation into Leo's involvement still ongoing?

But there was a more vital question he asked himself hundreds of times a day: because of the public profile of the Vacation Killer, by the time Vicky Cordingley was murdered in the UK, had so many people forwarded the Laura email that this time it had actually got back to the sender?

# CHAPTER 3

When he'd walked out of Chevalier's Bar without Laura, Leo's life changed beyond recognition and his job as project manager at TechFlex Industrial Design was the first casualty.

His firm of architects were as supportive as they could have been during the months following Laura's disappearance but there was only a certain amount of leave that could be compassionate. And with the possibility that Laura was still alive, Leo was surprised that his sporadic attendance due to the early police interrogations and his own intensive search didn't lead to a suspended then terminated contract sooner.

He'd played out every conceivable scenario in his head, knew the geography of the area where she'd vanished within a mile radius. Security footage from

Opallios hadn't revealed a glimpse of her after she'd left the building and street cameras from the adjacent high street hadn't captured anything significant either. If she'd been taken in a car he'd projected the route that would be impeded by the least traffic, the motorway it would eventually lead to and the possible destinations afterwards. He'd calculated that, even at lunchtime, she could have been out of London in less than forty-five minutes. He'd still have been sitting in the bar.

Hektor and his Chevalier's staff had been grilled — first by the police and then by Leo. The bar had only just opened for lunch and everyone had been getting ready for the midday rush. Nobody had even noticed Laura and Leo enter the premises.

Hektor had been angry with Leo because the investigation led to the exposure of several illegal immigrants working on his premises. But he'd known Laura long before Leo had, and she'd been drinking in Chevalier's years before she started at Opallios. So he'd softened enough to show Leo to the fire exit beyond the inner door to the ladies toilet. There was a small yard at the back of the premises but it was difficult to imagine someone gaining access, let alone taking Laura over the shards of glass cemented into the top of the wall.

The backdrop to that day seemed so commonplace but the idea of there being somebody, a face and a personality lurking within it that had orchestrated her sudden absence from his life forced him to consider every person he passed in the street, searching their eyes and wondering if they'd seen Laura since he had.

How and where had they lured her? What possible deception would she have fallen for? That was what he found harder to accept than anything else. They'd both occupied the same sensible reality that didn't allow for anything like this to happen.

And so the circuit of thought went unbroken and Leo envisaged a faceless observer in every crevice of every moment of that day. It was exhausting.

The couple had only just moved into a Victorian, mid-terrace house in Pimlico which they had planned to renovate together. After all they'd gone through to secure the place Leo was determined not to let it go; losing their home would have been unforgivable.

So he found a new job as security guard at Sable Electronics and although it barely paid the bills, his other living overheads were negligible. Working seven days of night shifts just about clawed in the monthly payment. He couldn't bear thinking about Laura's life insurance. As she was still missing, her assets were frozen for seven years. Seven years before she could be pronounced dead. Leo didn't even want to consider the implications of ever claiming.

Months passed. Months of waiting, of nurturing germs of hope. But even though the idea that Laura was still living and breathing somewhere became less likely, it still jabbed at his core with the same sickening urgency. It triggered him at any point of the day or night, a surge of adrenaline that almost brought him to his feet but at the same time left him feeling powerless to implement anything that he hadn't done a hundred times already.

Waiting was his illness but at least his new job allowed his non-participation in the life he had to carry on in the meantime. It also gave some order to his waking hours and a place to go – away from the leftover props of his museum home life – somewhere he could at least try to think.

As months dragged past, as the phone calls from the police ebbed, Leo looked for any way to maintain the urgency he felt to keep on looking.

Earlier in the year John Bookwalter had become the third American citizen to claim responsibility for the murders of the Vacation Killer. He'd given himself up to the New Orleans Police Department a couple of days after Louis Allan-Carlin's jawbone had been mailed to UK authorities and had been dismissed as a crank less than twenty-four hours later. Having never left the state of Louisiana during any of his thirty-eight years, he was the least likely candidate of the other cranks that had preceded him. The fact that none of the victims had been murdered in the state of Louisiana was also a detail that he treated as immaterial. He was the most vociferous of the would-be Vacation Killers though, protesting his guilt on his MySpace page before its popularity necessitated him registering a domain name.

The internet community, ever fond of embracing eccentrics and lunatics accorded him cult status and, at its peak, his website was generating twenty-three thousand hits a day.

It was Laura's older sister, Ashley, who told Leo about John Bookwalter. She was making her customary Thursday evening visit while he got ready to start his evening shift.

'I'm only telling you so you know what's out there. Don't go near his site.' She undid her black raincoat, releasing her anise scent into the room and leant against the kitchen dresser. The persistent rain had flattened her matte black hair, her usually perfectly coiffed curls hanging untidily around her face. In the glare of the kitchen lights, though, even the physical similarities couldn't approximate Laura. It was the playful vibrancy about the eyes that was missing. 'Promise me.' She picked up the steaming mug of coffee that he'd made her. He'd overfilled it and it slopped over the sides as she lifted it from the counter.

*If it doesn't drip on the floor, Laura is still alive.*

Most daily events, large or small, were yardsticks for Laura's well being. It was a compulsion that had begun eleven days after Laura had vanished and no parcel had been delivered to the police.

Leo's eyes darted between the bottom of the mug and

the circle of coffee it had left on the counter. Should he clean it up now? He'd become obsessive about keeping the house clean in anticipation of Laura's return.

'Leo?'

'I promise.' He straightened the security cap on his head. Leo never doubted that Ashley had been a woman since the age of eight and her no-nonsense intensity had always made Laura seem much younger than the three years that separated them. Ashley was a divorcee with a recent and obscenely generous settlement and the three of them had spent an uncharacteristic amount of time together just before Laura's disappearance, trying to rekindle Ashley's self-esteem as well as a dormant but promising sense of humour.

'So, it's still Christmas then?' Ashley nodded towards the hallway where the streamers that Leo had hung as a surprise for Laura on their return home from their shopping trip still remained. However consumed he had become by domestic cleanliness he still couldn't bring himself to remove the decorations or the Christmas tree, even after he'd hoovered up every one of the pine needles that it had shed onto the carpet. She softened. 'The place is still more spotless than mine though... and I have a cleaner.'

Leo and Ashley both knew that Laura had never cared for housework. It kept Leo busy though, on the rare occasions he wasn't using temazepam to sleep through the day.

Ashley opened a kitchen cupboard and surveyed the tins neatly stacked inside. 'You *are* eating?'

Leo ignored the questions. 'So what sort of things is this Bookwalter saying about Laura?'

Ashley's jaw tightened and she used the action of replacing her mug to avoid his eye.

Leo was relieved nothing had spilt from the mug to the tiles.

'He's a grubby little scumbag. Don't subject yourself to it.'

Leo had been surprised at how calmly Ashley had dealt with Laura's disappearance. She'd been midway through her divorce when Laura had been taken, however, and already reliant on tranquillisers. With so much to deal with, Leo had doubted that the self-confidence that he and Laura had been cultivating while she waited for her divorce settlement would return. It had, however, and he was glad for his sake as well as Laura's. He wondered how much of it was a performance for his benefit though.

'Anyway, you've promised me now.' She wiped the edges of her purple-glossed lips with her purple-glossed nails.

Leo had never been particularly close to Ashley, even after he married Laura. However, they both now shared an excruciating and open cavity in their lives that most other people couldn't understand. Both his parents were dead and the rest of Laura's family had distanced themselves when he had become a suspect. His brother, Matty, was absent when he really needed him but that was customary.

Ashley pumped him for more reassurances that he wouldn't go near the internet and then kissed him goodbye. After he'd seen her off he wondered if he took her regular visits for granted now and thought about how much he'd miss them if they stopped. He returned to the kitchen, washed his mug, dried it and returned it to its place before wiping the ring off the counter.

Leo sat on his bed, his laptop booted and resting on his crossed legs. He entered Laura's name into a Google search. With his life devoid of her for so long he was stunned when he hit 'Images'. Her face was suddenly smiling back at him from a page full of thumbnails. He felt emotions he'd kept carefully in check stabbing the back of his throat and then trickling down into his stomach.

Most of the pictures he recognised as the ones he and her parents had pulled out of boxes and albums and printed off discs to supply to the police – private captured moments now used for consumption by the public domain. But one of them he didn't recognise at all.

It was this picture that led him to Bookwalter's site – a photo of Laura when she was about seventeen, wearing an oversized T-shirt tugged over her legs and pulling her hair across her mouth.

And when he found the photo of Laura's youth, the strand of henna hair held under her nose like a moustache and the eyes of a Laura who had yet to look upon him, he felt for the first time that she was no longer his.

The void that had been gradually swelling inside him expanded further and compacted the hopelessness and guilt.

# CHAPTER 4

In the months that followed Laura's disappearance the mere thought of subjecting himself to what the internet customarily threw up out of human misery was inconceivable.

But he couldn't forget the Vacation Killer's email, the one that had described Vicky Cordingley before police had received the parcel containing her jawbone. He'd reported it to IT but he hadn't forwarded it. Would Vicky Cordingley have died if he hadn't broken the chain? If she hadn't did that mean that Laura would still be with him? He doubted it but despite statistical probability it continued to afflict him.

He wondered if it was his guilt about not forwarding the Vicky Cordingley email that made him go to Bookwalter's site and send a message.

Skipping the home page he clicked straight on *Contact vk*. He explained who he was and asked not only that the picture of Laura be removed from the site but also demanded to know exactly where Bookwalter had obtained it. It seemed obscene that a complete stranger on the other side of the world possessed a personal photo of Laura – a photo Leo had never seen before – and was using her image like a character in an online game.

Moments later his inbox told him he had mail and he momentarily expected to find that the email had been undelivered. But it was an email from Bookwalter. It was chillingly familiar and only one new line had been added at the top.

*You mustve missed this. Am forwarding again.*

*howdy doody,*

*still in the uk*

*tall, freckle faced, chicken pox scar on left eyebrow*

*forward this email to ten friends*

*each of those friends must forward it to ten friends*

*maybe one of those friends of friends of friends will be one of my friends*

*if this email ends up in my inbox within a week I wont slit the bitchs throat*

*can you afford not to send this on to ten friends?*

*vk*

Leo stared at the email for a long time, listening to his own breathing.

Bookwalter's website (*stillonvacation.com*) was an accomplished and professional enterprise that obviously had the input of well-paid designers. His splash entry page was a mosaic of sensational front-page headlines that outlined the significant episodes of his supposed crimes. Between the visitor counter (1,112,158) and the revolving Enter button was one headline that Leo assumed Bookwalter had mocked up himself:

## JOHN R BOOKWALTER:
## RELEASED INTO SOCIETY

The fact that he'd been released into society after less than a day of police questioning was probably lost on many of his visitors and when you clicked through to his home page no mention of this fact was evident.

Bookwalter's photograph was far more flattering than the media images circulated at the time of his surrender to the police. But it still couldn't hide the left-handed squint which made it look as if he'd spent his entire life peering through a telescope. A flat black cloth cap covered his head and a few auburn fronds were evident around his ears. His appearance was that of an avuncular bachelor whom Leo could imagine owning a saxophone. He was far from serial killer material but he supposed that that was the one facet that made him convincing.

There was a regular blog page which was Bookwalter's platform for sneering at the media and authorities, a forum for his visitors to ask him questions and debate amongst themselves and a links page to countless other serial killer fan sites which all fed off each other's morbidity.

At a glance Leo could tell that the visitors and forum regulars on Bookwalter's site ran the gamut from the obsessive to the ghoulish. He guessed most of them were probably teenagers. To most, John Bookwalter appeared to be a figure of fun whom they enjoyed indulging and it was easy to see how their cult hero worship and make-believe had stoked the pseudo folklore even further.

A brief but inflated précis of the crimes he claimed as his own followed the photo and below this, separated by animated blood gushes, was a list of dates with photos of the victims. The photos could be clicked on so you could view a profile and more intimate details of their dispatch. Leo hovered the cursor over Laura's photo but then clicked on Louis Allan-Carlin. The text was obviously lifted from media reports to which Bookwalter added his own haughty contributions in brackets.

On December 30th 2007, a boiled and polished jawbone *(arduous but satisfying work)* belonging to twenty-five-year-old Louis Allan-Carlin was posted to Surrey police headquarters in the UK and a search was launched for the remains of his body. Undoubtedly a victim of the Vacation Killer, his disappearance had been preceded by a much-circulated email that authorities assumed to be describing a potential 'blonde' female victim *(inspirational police work)*. However, because of the lack of detail and the volume of similar hoax emails being sent at the time, the police were powerless to prevent the murder. Louis Allan-Carlin's body has never been found *(only the wallflowers know).*

Ironically, the wealthy parents of Louis Allan-Carlin, Jo and Maggie, had previously issued a reward for information regarding the disappearance of an employee at Opallios, their jointly owned company. Laura Sharpe vanished a week before they last saw their son *(an impulse Christmas acquisition?)* However, police speculated as to whether the two incidents were related or if the Vacation Killer was using the Allan-Carlins to make a statement about the investigation going off track *(more keen-edged speculation).* No remains of Laura Sharpe have ever been posted or discovered *(theres madness in my method).*

As Leo clicked the photos of Teresa Strickland and Vicky Cordingley he noticed how elusive Bookwalter was about the UK murders. Bookwalter had admitted to both Laura and Louis' disappearances but he seemed to take less delight in outlining the UK episodes – choosing to be cryptic and elusive and playing down his own interest. Leo wondered if it was because, having never left the US, Bookwalter didn't have a handle on an environment he'd never visited.

When Leo eventually summoned up the courage to click through to Laura's profile it merely re-stated the facts of her disappearance to which Bookwalter only added one comment.

*(Never to be found?)*

The site told him that Bookwalter was online to do a Q&A forum and Leo registered and logged in. He threatened him with a suit he wasn't even sure he could bring and was poleaxed by the reply that quickly followed.

*If you are who you say you are – when did you first meet Laura Sharpe?*

The last thing he'd expected was for a delusional like Bookwalter to question *his* validity. Sharpe was his name, the one that Laura had gladly adopted. The idea that a faceless community had seized upon it and become protective of it purely in connection to Laura made him feel a worse isolation than he'd experienced during the police interrogations. His curiosity as to whether anyone else would know the answer to the question, however, overrode his reflex to slam the lid of his laptop.

*2007.*

He entered the numbers, hit return then unstuck his fingertips from the keyboard as quickly as he could.

He'd already felt like he was cheapening his own suspended grief, as well as that of Laura's family, the instant he'd logged onto the site but this moment of justifying himself to John Bookwalter made him realise how desperate he'd become. Suddenly, inexplicably, every minute he'd lived and breathed with Laura, since they'd first met while helping move a mutual friend into his new flat, felt like it hinged on Bookwalter's approval. He waited and felt his circulation burning his ears.

*Would you like a 1-2-1? Come into my private lounge area and chat. Will email the password.*

He did.

*Password: howdydoody*

Leo felt his stomach curling up into his ribcage but his finger was already clicking the cursor on the left-hand column and entering the password. Sat alone on his bed it seemed surreal that he was about to exchange dialogue about his wife with a stranger on the other side of the Atlantic. He tried to imagine Bookwalter sat at his own computer and fought the urge to yank the power cable from his laptop.

*You there Leo?*

*Leo?*

Leo imagined his correspondent waiting. He gripped the edges of his screen and felt the muscles in his wrist tauten as he prepared to close the lid. But Bookwalter was persistent and Leo watched his methodic letters fill the screen again.

*Laura says hi.*

# CHAPTER 5

On April 2$^{nd}$ 2008, Howard Bonsignore, a travelling sales rep for Gristex cattle feed products, already arrested for the murder of Tom Andrutti, admitted to all the Vacation Killer murders as well as the murders of two male prostitutes which he claimed to have committed in Montenegro. These were never confirmed and details of his sporadic American interstate movements were also sketchy. However, his Gristex company itinerary confirmed his presence in Montenegro but more importantly in Germany and the UK at the most relevant times and it seemed that was all that was necessary. Authorities buckling under pressure from all sides welcomed his timely candour. The murders ceased but then they had for nearly three months before Bonsignore opened his mouth.

And after that the case snapped shut, revealing little else of value to the victims' families while Bonsignore revelled in the ongoing enigma. The locations of the bodies remaining unidentified.

The British police were as sceptical about Bonsignore's confession as Leo, and even after the convict's confession to all the murders including Laura's, Leo still saw the cars in his street. He knew it was partly his own paranoia but he was positive that some of the time he was still being watched by the police. It was something that he'd grown accustomed to, however, and he convinced himself that their presence would eventually bear out his innocence.

* * *

Eleven months after his confession, Bonsignore awoke to the buzz of the motorised lock on his cell. He was always the last to eat and already it felt like the acid in his empty stomach was eating him alive. He was sure the guards made him wait longer and longer each day. As he swung his legs off the bunk, he wondered which scraps would be left for him this time. He hadn't even been able to identify yesterday's meal.

One of the new guards was waiting for him at the end of the corridor tonight. He'd only been working at Baraga for a couple of weeks. Hadn't even started shaving. They were both pieces of white trash; only age and a uniform separated them. Bonsignore could tell that he frightened the new kid though and tried to meet his eye as he passed. The boy looked at his shoes as he waited to lock the door again. Bonsignore took a long look at him and inhaled – cheap soap and popcorn – just enough to recharge the fantasy about him he'd been using at night. He dreamt more about the boy than he did about bloody doorsteps of rib-eye steak. The door was closed quickly behind him and he ambled slowly down to the canteen block, tugging on the growth of hair under his bottom lip.

When he reached the crossroads at the end of that corridor Bonsignore was suddenly aware that something wasn't right. There was too much sound bouncing back at him and he realised that some of the other prisoners had still to return to their cells. There was a long line of them passing from his left to his right and he instinctively took a step backwards to allow them to pass. The guards knew better than to mix him with the others; what the fuck were they playing at? He liked them to believe that he hated taking his meals alone but it was actually something he looked on as a privilege. The brawls he'd instigated in the past had afforded him the isolation he wanted but they'd mis-timed the mealtimes tonight and he suddenly felt vulnerable.

*For a moment Bonsignore was clutching the rusty wires of the tree swing he'd used to jump off of naked into the creek when he was seven, could feel the abrasion of the steel in his young palms and the smoothness of the wooden seat as he let go. There was no splash though – just a pop sound as if someone had squeezed some bubble pack in his ear.*

Then the object that had been shoved into his eyeball released the clear aqueous fluid inside it before piercing further into his brain. His memory disconnected from his considerable weight and he folded to the floor like a paper lantern.

\* \* \*

Leo heard Laura murmur something to him as if she was half asleep, then made that sound she always did with her tongue against the roof of her mouth. He felt her henna hair on his face and smelt and felt her breath about his top lip. Then the phone punched through the temazepam and he didn't know if he'd been asleep for an hour or a minute. He looked at the telephone for a while and marvelled at how long the person on the other end was waiting for an answer. Whoever it was knew what it took.

*If they ring off before I can reach it, Laura is alive.*

He picked up.

'Leo. It's Matty...' Small talk was no currency.

'I was asleep.' Leo said through his nostrils.

'Thought I'd swing by.'

That woke Leo up. 'When?' He played for time while he tried to think of an excuse.

'Today.'

'I have to sleep today. I'm still on nights.'

46

'I'm sitting in my car outside your house. Open up.' Matty hung up to underline the victory.

Leo opened the curtain, peered at Matty's Lexus parked at the end of the drive and did a customary scan for a police surveillance car. There were none parked in the street that looked familiar. He was sure the police regularly switched cars though. Then he caught his own thirty-year-old features in the glass and noticed how they coordinated with the grey morning outside. Although his newly grown dark moustache was neatly trimmed, his excavated expression jarred with the sharp symmetry of his closely shaved hair. He'd never worn it as short when Laura had been around. She'd always said she'd fancy him with a moustache and a number one but he'd never been keen.

He guessed that it was now some time within the hours of respectable nine to five and noticed he was still dressed in his security uniform from the night before. He padded down the stairs and opened the door to an expression of stifled exasperation that he was more than accustomed to finding on his younger brother's face. Matty was about to insert a key into the lock and Leo chided himself for having given Matty the duplicate key when he and Laura had needed somebody to water the plants.

Matty hadn't changed since they were kids and still sported the tight brown curls and the flaring nostrils

47

that had attracted a lot of unkind ribbing at school. There was only two years between them but there was nothing in their features to tie them by blood. So much so that, as a child, Leo had wondered if they'd been adopted.

Matty was clutching some brown paper take-out bags under his arm. 'Like your hair that length.' Matty must have read somewhere that you should always try to start every conversation by saying something positive even if it was untrue. His second statement pushed crabbily to the front of the queue, however. 'What took you so long?'

'I had to get dressed.' Leo answered.

Matty didn't wait to be invited in and ducked under the arm that Leo had deliberately left between his body and the door handle. Leo shut the door and scraped up some mail off the wooden tiles, turning to find him in the kitchen unpacking some wrapped food from the bag. Outwardly confident and take-control Matty. How quickly things had turned around. 'You brought us breakfast?' He followed him to exert some damage control.

'Brunch. There's dozens of wholefood places around here. Have you any idea how long it took me to find a café selling good old-fashioned filth?' Matty dumped the grease-spotted bags on the counter and garnished them with a couple of sauce sachets and scrunched up napkins.

Leo quickly lifted them off the counter and felt his stomach muscles lock when he saw the shiny stains they'd left. He opened a cupboard and felt the same sensation as he pulled out two side plates from the neat stack inside. He dumped the bags on them. He could wash them up and return them to the stack immediately after Matty left.

'Ciggy.' Matty made for the back door and unlocked it so he could stand on the balcony overlooking the small, gravelled garden.

It irritated Leo that Matty never had a cigarette on his way over. It meant he had to stand out there with him in the cold.

'How's things?' Matty exhaled smoke through it matter-of-factly, as if it weren't as significant as everyone who asked it of Leo.

'Working a lot.'

'Too much maybe?'

Leo was in no mood for Matty's new caring, sharing persona. 'So, are you on your way somewhere?'

'Got a few things to do in town. I did make the journey to see you though.' He narrowed his eyes into the distance for effect. 'Thought you'd like some company on your birthday.' Another victory.

The mail was still in Leo's hands. He'd wondered why there'd been a few more coloured envelopes than usual. 'It's very thoughtful of you, Matty. I've got plans already though,' he lied.

'Corresponding with your internet lunatic?' He changed tack as soon as he registered Leo's lips harden. 'Why don't you get some time off and come over to see us. We could book somewhere.'

'Us' meant Carla and the twins. Carla had a sparkling smile and intelligence that she seemed to have distributed evenly between her children. Leo missed playing with them. Missed improvising assault courses for them in the back garden. 'Difficult to get the time off at the moment. Maybe we could arrange to do something over the next couple of weeks.'

Matty filled his chest with air as if girding himself for the usual date commitment tussle. 'Molly and Greg haven't seen you in ages.'

'I know. I did call in for their birthdays.' He recalled how they'd both clung to his legs as he'd left.

'That was August.' Matty jigged his foot between the bottom of the railing.

'Let me have a look at the rota.'

'Look, everyone's concerned about you, OK?' Matty turned and made significant eye contact with him. 'Everyone.'

It was a good performance but Leo knew it was just Matty acting in a way he knew he was supposed to. He was learning and it was well intentioned, but Leo just couldn't take it coming from him.

'Let me have a look at the rota when I go in tonight.'

'OK, but phone us tomorrow. I'm telling them you're coming, OK?'

Leo was relieved that it was once again down to the vagaries of telephones and missed calls. He waved Matty off soon after.

*If he doesn't beep the horn then she's not in pain.*

Matty did.

# CHAPTER 6

Cleaves watched Matty pull away from the house and
Leo closing the front door. He'd seen Matty visit him
before but registered that it had been some time since
his last social call. Now Leo was inside again he put the
fan on to clear the condensation from the windscreen.

Leo's existence seemed to follow the same pattern.
Work, sleep, clean the house, interspersed with sporadic
visits to the supermarket and the barber's. It looked like
another carbon-copy surveillance day. And as Cleaves
tore off half a stick of breakfast gum and chewed it in
the side of his jaw that didn't ache, he didn't suspect
that the next twenty-four hours would compromise the
position and identity he'd carefully maintained for all
the months he'd been watching Leo.

* * *

Leo glanced around the seventies décor of the living room. It was now fifteen months since Laura had vanished and nothing had changed. The Christmas streamers were still up and the pea-green walls still sported blotches of test pot paint, the winning colour's re-enforcements purchased and waiting unopened in tins under the stairs. Everything was now more pristine and polished than it had ever been when Laura had lived here but it wasn't right that he should finish their colour scheme alone.

The house was nothing more than a routinely maintained showroom but it reminded him that Laura was still unmistakably present. Not just in the photos of them together that hung from walls and stood on the cupboard and TV unit. Everything echoed her, from the layout of the room to the empty, handmade fruit bowl in the middle of the dining table that had her name kiln-fired into the bottom.

He felt a heaviness in his head and realised that his breathing had got louder. The prescription sleeping pills had waited patiently for his brother to leave but now the adrenaline had ebbed they were demanding his full attention.

He lingered though; feeling like he'd broken into someone else's house, and Laura observed him from all angles. She wasn't the most successful photographer's subject; her dark brown eyes were slightly narrowed by a stagy, lopsided smile in all the pictures. However the gentle mischief that played above the band of freckles that extended in a strip across the bridge of her nose was present in all of them. And when he looked at her laughing he could hear her peculiar way of not laughing, the sound trapping in her throat and her shoulders silently quaking.

He headed for bed but when he got there he swung the laptop onto this knees.

*Password: howdy doody*

\* \* \*

Doctor Mutatkar sat with his family at dinner but heard none of what was being said. It was a common state of affairs and he'd long learnt how to disguise it. It used to be easier. With such a workload his wife was quick to blame his preoccupation on the pressures of his job but lately she sat opposite and waited for him to emerge from his reveries with a look that probably mirrored his.

His mind was still in the other place, the place he'd much rather be right now. The TV news had rekindled a dread that he thought he'd got used to but which was still waiting for him as keenly and as undiluted as it had on those days directly after what had happened.

The room closed around the faces in his foreground and when he avoided their eyes he was looking at a plate of food that he knew he couldn't force himself to eat.

He excused himself and, feeling his wife's eyes on him, walked as calmly as he could out of the room and headed to the downstairs toilet — but his cheeks burnt even in the cool atmosphere there.

He caught himself in the mirror, something he'd been avoiding for some time. He wondered what his wife saw when she looked at him. She'd stopped telling him the lines on his fifty-five-year-old features were distinguished anymore but she was the last person to stop recognising him. He'd not been able to for years.

He felt the weight of the deception as if it hung in a heavy bag hooked to his stomach. He lifted the seat to vomit.

* * *

Leo ground another meal to paste and surveyed four corridors from eight different angles. He looked at the tortilla wrap in his hand to remind himself what he was eating and waited for the black and white images on the monitors in front of him to change. They did at the exact second he knew they would. He didn't even have to count now; his brain was completely attuned to their rhythm.

The cleaners would be coming in soon. His body clock told him this because he felt suddenly alert and it was just at the end of his shift that he was the most awake. With the effects of the pills completely wearing off it lasted about half an hour before he could get home and swallow some more.

He wondered how pleased his employers would be to know that he dozed and hallucinated for the majority of his shift but woke up when there were other employees in the building.

The images on the screen changed again.

*If a cleaner appears in the next five seconds it means Laura's dead.*

Leo held his breath but no figure appeared. He felt a slight relief as he breathed out. The darker perspective of the shadowy warehouse fire exits highlighted the reflection of his sun-starved features. Ashley said he lacked Vitamin D and had bought him a canister of supplements. Figuring his insides probably already resembled a chalk landscape, he'd never taken any.

Moments of clarity, that's what he hated about the last half hour. He used to have a nightmare when he was a kid. It was about somebody breaking in through the back door. The frosted pane revealed only the dark shape of the intruder but the worst part was not only that he couldn't move as the rattles of the handle became more aggressive, but that his eyes felt like they could only open a crack as he struggled to glimpse the figure as the door opened. He never did see the intruder but nowadays it was being able to open his eyes that brought him the closest to panic.

He pictured Matty talking to Carla while the twins dangled from him and him telling her about his visit to Leo and how he'd tried his best. He tried not to imagine

Molly and Greg's disappointment. They were sweet kids but Leo didn't trust himself not to disappoint them for real. The medication affected his moods but he knew it was more about trying to keep his patience in check with Matty rather than the kids. It annoyed Leo that Matty pretended to be their real father when actually he had only inherited the perfect family, refusing to acknowledge the spectre of Carla's ex and the fact that she'd brought them up perfectly well before he'd sidled onto the scene.

He peered past his reflection and into the shadows of the warehouse and felt a familiar sensation of inertia – waiting for something that wasn't about to happen. Then the phone rang. It rarely did and its strident sound kick-started his circulation.

'Security?'

'Leo?'

He recognised the dried out husk of her voice immediately. 'Hello, Maggie.'

'I'm so sorry. I tried your home number.' Nowadays, Maggie Allan-Carlin always sounded apologetic. 'Are you in the middle of something?'

'No, what's wrong?' Something had to be.

'It's Bonsignore.'

Leo hadn't heard the name for a good while but his brain had turned it over so many times that it still sounded threadbare. 'What about him?'

'He's dead.'

# CHAPTER 7

Without changing out of his uniform, Leo drove straight to the Allan-Carlins. Their palatial house was on the border of Shere, a small commuter-belt village outside London. His normal daily drive necessitated covering under a mile from Sable Electronics to his home on mainly empty roads so he'd been nervous about driving such a distance after a shift.

Far from puncturing his exhaustion the news had left him as detached as he had been at the end of Bonsignore's trial and, as the rain on the windscreen of the Saab got heavier, he resisted the temptation to turn on the wipers. Their rhythm had almost been fatal in the past – for him and other road users. He checked his rear-view mirror for a car but couldn't remember what the colour of the last police surveillance vehicle had been.

He speculated as to who would be sitting on the low leather sofa at the back of Chevalier's at that very moment and then realised that probably nobody would at this hour of the morning. How many people would sit in that spot today though, the seat where he'd waited? How many would use the ladies restroom? A familiar treadmill of thought cranked to life.

As the A3 took him through Epsom and he hadn't identified any car as having accompanied him all the way, Leo realised that the last journey he'd made of any length was to the same location. He'd visited the Allan-Carlins at their home on a handful of significant occasions. A visit to Maggie and Joe was always a reminder of a shared loss but it was patently clear that it was only Maggie who willingly entertained his presence.

She'd told him to come at once so they could watch things unfold on the news and if he wasn't so indebted to them he certainly wouldn't have been driving barely conscious along the wet and hazardous roads. He swung the car sharply into the turning that led off the A3 and zigzagged up the forest track that led to their impressive, Georgian home. To an outsider, it appeared that life had been very kind to the Allan-Carlins.

Lights were on in every window and the door to their garage glided open as he pulled in front of the house. He parked the car and Maggie appeared through the side door. There was another marked decline in her appearance and it shocked even Leo. How long had it been since his last visit? It could only have been a matter of months. Now, her usually meticulously applied make-up was absent and her dark hair lay in uncombed disarray around her shoulders. Her complexion was as bloodless as his and served to highlight any blemishes. She wore loose-fitting, turquoise, fleece leisurewear and a pair of bright green crocs – he noticed her left hand was bandaged. She gave him a fragile smile as he got out of the car.

*If Maggie hugs me it means Laura is still breathing.*

Maggie put her good arm around him. She held him there without saying anything like she always did and he could smell the stale sweetness of alcohol – it wasn't yet 9 a.m. Finally, she released him so he could follow her indoors.

The door from the garage led directly into a brightly lit, tiled kitchen where Joe was scraping up broken fragments of crockery with a dustpan and brush. He looked up through his bushy grey eyebrows and nodded once at Leo. A ring of white hair clung to the sides of his head and a sprig under his nose sheltered from the rest of his patent baldness, but the only change Leo noted in Joe's appearance was that he appeared to have shrunk a little more. He didn't know if this was his imagination though because Joe's presence was usually peripheral, circling Leo's visits from a distance or standing in adjoining rooms with a tumbler of brandy until he left. His head was bright red, and Leo suspected he'd interrupted an argument. He was dressed more crisply then Maggie – polo shirt, chinos and canvas shoes and it was obvious from his previous visits that Joe was the designated stay-in-control party of the relationship. Joe still ran Opallios but Leo assumed he now held it together on his own.

'Sorry about the mess. I seem to be getting clumsier,' Maggie rasped as she breezed past her husband. Joe rolled his eyes at her as she passed and it was obvious that she had given him a look. 'Coffee?'

'Please.' It seemed like a good idea if he was to attempt the drive back.

'Futile for me to offer you something stronger...' Maggie put the spout of the kettle under the tap.

'Coffee's fine.'

Joe dumped the shards of crockery in the bin but didn't beat his customary retreat.

'We've got Fox News on in the lounge. They're giving it more coverage.' She clumsily plugged in the kettle and flicked the switch, then picked up a large tumbler of amber liquid and ice. She'd never drunk alcohol in front of him before. 'Have you seen any of it yet?'

'I came straight here.'

'Come on then.' The words scratched at her throat as Maggie chinked into the lounge. Leo followed and was surprised to hear Joe behind him.

The Allan-Carlins' lounge was decorated with impractical coral carpets and white showroom furniture showing inevitable signs of neglect. Surely they had people coming in to clean? To his right the floor-to-ceiling windows showcased the acres of land that lay beyond the covered swimming pool, now coated by a crust of dead leaves. But as always their attention was focused on the enormous flat-screen TV that hung on the back wall; it was permanently turned on during his visits.

The three of them stood in front of it and waited, watching a report about Egyptian troops being deployed along the Gaza-Egypt border and eyeing the crawler at the bottom of the screen. Although he'd only just got out of the car, Leo's knees sagged from exhaustion and he had to keep snapping them straight to prevent him from tipping forward.

'I'll sit if that's OK.' He pulled out a high-backed chair from the dining table display and awkwardly spun it round so it faced the screen. It took more effort to sit in it than to stand.

Joe moved into his line of vision to close the curtains, then Bonsignore's elongated features filled the screen. Fox were still using the same photograph of Bonsignore that every news station had throughout the trial; the one that had been taken of him with his fishing buddies, the face of the person standing next to him blurred out. A floppy blue denim hat sat at the top of his extended forehead. His eyes were slits, squinted against the sun and he was grinning.

*Howard Bonsignore, otherwise known as the Vacation Killer, died in Baraga Maximum Correctional Facility today after being assaulted by fellow inmate, Jacob Frank. Bonsignore, serving twelve life sentences for a spate of brutal killings which he carried out across seven US states as well as two corroborated European locations, was treated at the Brooks Medical Centre but died from brain trauma after he was stabbed in the eye with an unspecified weapon. With only months of his sentence served, relatives of Bonsignore's victims are asking how this could have happened when the convicted killer should have been housed in a segregated unit. Jacob Frank was only midway through serving four consecutive sentences for aggravated assault.*

The picture changed to a circling helicopter's view of Baraga.

*Warden Greg King has spoken only to confirm details of the event... Bonsignore never revealed the locations of most of his victims' bodies and was still key to ongoing investigations.*

Leo estimated Bonsignore to be nearly forty now. He'd confessed to killing twelve women and six men. His last victim had been Tom Andrutti, his own long-term boyfriend. Bonsignore still seemed like a fictional character – white, wannabe alpha male and the subject of an international manhunt that culminated in his confession to the Vacation Killer murders after murdering Andrutti. The trial and the media hype surrounding it had unfolded from a place that Leo had felt entirely dislocated from.

The three of them watched the same report book-ending the rest of the day's news stories before Joe switched off the TV with the remote. The crackling screen seemed to pick up the static in the room and even Maggie's neurosis couldn't fill the silence.

'That's it then,' Joe said definitively, although he seemed to be waiting for a consensus.

Leo suddenly felt his wrist straining with the weight of the full coffee mug in his hand and he couldn't remember when it had been placed there.

'Thanks for coming to see Maggie.' Joe left after he said it and Leo knew he wasn't just thanking him for driving to their house that morning. He was thanking him for all his visits now that no more would be required.

Leo looked at Maggie but she didn't make eye contact. 'Is this enough for you?'

'Of course not,' she croaked eventually and then lubricated her throat with her glass. 'It's always been out of our hands, though. You know that don't you.' She still didn't meet his gaze but fixed her eyes on the patch of wall beneath the TV.

'There's so much we never found out.'

'And what more would we have learnt if he'd lived another twenty years? Or wanted to learn?' She clicked her wedding ring nervously against the side of the glass.

Of course, things were different for Maggie and Joe. There were more absolutes for them. It was obviously how Joe saw it but Maggie had been closer to Laura.

Maggie didn't take his arm as she normally did when he left but led the way to the garage, striding as if she were trying to beat her own emotions.

'I had another sitting last Friday. She's in a comfortable place now,' she said as she hugged his shirt collar again.

'Maggie.' Joe's muffled remonstration came from the other side of the door. He must have followed them back into the kitchen.

Maggie touched Leo's cheek, found his eyes and shuttered out her green tears. She nodded and returned to her husband.

# CHAPTER 8

'Events have made her embrace things that normally she wouldn't have got mixed up in.'

It was what Joe had once said about Maggie's involvement with a local spiritualist. There was always a deluded message of reassurance for Leo when he left but, driving back, he realised how much he was going to miss them.

He knew that contact with the Allan-Carlins would be short-lived after Bonsignore had been convicted. He couldn't blame them for wanting to move on and had noticed that the photographs of Louis about their home had slowly dwindled. Now there was only a single frame of photos in the hallway showing him growing up from a baby to the age of twenty-five. He wasn't being forgotten but his school portraits and university achievements had obviously become too much of a painful reminder to have hanging on display every day.

Did Leo really have an implicit connection to Bonsignore and the Allan-Carlin's grief? Bonsignore's confession to Laura's disappearance suggested so. But now Joe had decided to sever his visits he'd shut down Leo's last palpable connection to the Vacation Killer. He suddenly felt twice removed from ever finding out where Laura had been taken and why the police had never been sent her parcel.

The rain had eased and, after looking both ways, Leo pulled the car out of the junction that would take him along the usually quiet stretch that led back to the A3.

The bike impacted before he'd pulled into the left lane, clipping his rear wing and spinning its rider around the axis of its front wheel.

The front of the Saab was spun back into the left lane where it came to rest and Leo saw the rider and his bike sliding on the hissing tarmac until they hit the muddied bank of trees to the left of the junction. It felt as if his seat belt was holding his rib cage together but he quickly unfastened it and got out of the car, jogging halfway over to where the rider lay. Pain bear-hugged his chest but before he reached the rider, another car leaving the same junction as Leo broke hard, hitting the back of the Saab with enough impact to smash the headlights.

He turned from one to the other and then held up his hand to the car driver before continuing to where the bike rider lay. He was already sitting up and snapping up his visor.

*If he's not injured, Laura hasn't been either.*

'Jesus, I'm so sorry. Anything broken?'

The rider lifted his visor and examined the snagged leather palms of his blue driving gloves. Leo registered that the boy was barely old enough to hold a licence. 'I don't think so.' His pale blue eyes shifted and he looked more embarrassed than anything else. He had to have been going full throttle but Leo wasn't sure he would have seen him even if the boy had been driving at normal speed. He couldn't trust his eyeballs and driving up he'd already experienced moments that felt like they were coming unglued from his frazzled brain cells. There was no way he should have been behind the wheel of a car and even though the impact had momentarily galvanised him he could already feel the shadows creeping back around the periphery of the accident scene.

'I think I'm OK.' It was looking more certain; the rider's attention had already turned to the state of his bike.

'Can you stand?' Leo helped him to his feet but the boy disengaged himself from his grip to demonstrate that he was perfectly capable of limping over to where his machine lay. He pulled his bike upright and examined the buckled front mudguard. Leo tried to ascertain the damage to the front of the other mud-spattered metallic olive car behind him. It looked OK...from the side anyway.

'I don't mind if you don't want to make this official.' There was a note of desperation in the rider's voice and he was already climbing back into the seat.

Leo guessed he was probably uninsured, had a healthy amount of points on his licence or didn't even possess one. 'As long as you're OK. Are you sure you wouldn't rather I call an ambulance or phone somebody to pick you up?'

The boy unsuccessfully kick-started the bike and a twinge registered on his face. 'No, it's cool.'

Leo knew the boy would be gone in a matter of seconds. 'Look, take it easy. As long as you're OK we can handle this however you want.'

The boy tried again but it was the car behind them that revved to life.

Leo turned in time to see the car that had come from behind him skid sideways and barrel down the road away from them. He squinted after the car but barely registered the model let alone the registration number.

Leo drove the rest of the way home in the slow lane, his gut shivering and rattling his bruised ribcage. He had all the windows open to keep him awake and had decided to stop at the first motel he came to. But as he got closer and closer to home without spotting one it seemed pointless to stop a few miles from his own bed.

He drove into a curtain of rain and large droplets thudded off the car seats. He hadn't even glimpsed the face of the driver in the metallic olive car, just a dark shape behind the windscreen's reflection of grey clouds. Perhaps they'd wanted to leave the scene for similar reasons to the boy on the motorcycle but Leo doubted it. It was a saloon car, Passat or Volvo and even though the side of it had been caked in mud it looked to have been brand new. Although he kept an eye out, he didn't glimpse it for the rest of the journey home but couldn't shake the notion that, if it had ever ceased, the surveillance was certainly underway again.

* * *

*Howdy Doody. Knew youd be in touch. Soon as I saw Howard Bonsignore on the news. So glad you did. Been worried about you.*

Leo always tried to imagine a New Orleans drawl behind the words on his laptop. He'd been contemplating having this dialogue for the few hours he'd been home. He tried sleeping but could almost feel the pressure of the daylight against the curtains. Leo had finally given up and switched on the TV instead. But Bonsignore's story had already been relegated from the mainstream channels. He'd sat up and lifted the laptop onto the bed but even as he hinged its lid open and then shut it the customary number of times before logging on, he knew his dialogue with Bookwalter was inevitable. He'd promised Ashley he wouldn't so many times but today had changed all that.

*You there Leo?*

The words never rattled out at a fast pace; Bookwalter was clearly a one-fingered typist. But even though the construction of the sentences was painstaking to watch, there was never a pause before his responses started filling the screen. Leo always got the impression that Bookwalter's impatience wasn't helped by his inability to type his own words fast enough.

Leo's keyboard expertise at least accelerated the pace of their exchanges. He crossed his legs tighter under the laptop and keyed in the first words he'd exchanged with him for over three weeks.

*Sorry to have been out of touch.*

*Understand. Have been busy with desalination plant protest.*

Leo's mind went blank but soon he could sense his correspondent's agitation. Sensing his time was up he stabbed quickly at one key:

*?????*

*Long story. Coordinating local opposition to proposed site. Website has just gone live. Log on to www. DesalAvert.com for figures relating to environmental impact of vacuum distillation.*

*Will take a look when I have some time.*

*Already have over 17,000 signatories on the petition. If you wouldnt mind taking a few moments Id be grateful.*

Just like the emails that had been circulated by the Vacation Killer, Bookwalter didn't use apostrophes. However, sometimes he slipped, as if his genuine grasp of punctuation got the better of him.

*Will be happy to. How are things otherwise?*

*Much obliged. Gastric flu doing the rounds here but have so far escaped. Laura says hi.*

Leo had wondered if Bookwalter's energies had shifted focus in the few weeks since he'd spoken to him but watching her name appearing on his screen shrink-wrapped everything to the space he occupied on the bed like it had the first time he'd discussed her with him.

*Is she well?*

*As can be expected.*

Sensitively, Bookwalter had agreed to remove all photos of Laura from her profile page so the only image that remained was the one on the home page that had been used by the media during her initial disappearance. This was on the condition that Leo would continue to correspond although he wasn't sure if Bookwalter would ever have offered to withdraw them if Laura hadn't been the Vacation Killer victim with the biggest question mark. She seemed to muddy the water for him and it seemed convenient to discard her. Or perhaps Bookwalter was worried about getting sued. However, judging by the increasing amount of banners and pop-ups on the site, he assumed that Bookwalter had to be making good on the revenue from the advertisers.

But although he'd been quick to remove the picture of Laura as a teenager, he would never be drawn on where he'd got it in the first place. Leo didn't want to consider how many hard drives it had already been saved on. The idea of the image being in global circulation and that computer-bound sociopaths were using them as currency was something he gladly would have committed murder for himself.

Leo stabbed at the keys.

*Was wondering what Laura's reaction to news is. Have you told her about Bonsignore?*

*You know better than that Leo.*

# CHAPTER 9

'Where have you been?'

Doctor Mutatkar barely registered his wife's question as he climbed the stairs. He was sure he answered but not what he said. Whatever it was he wasn't followed into the bedroom where he knelt on the floor looking at the telephone on the bedside table.

He couldn't stop it now, even if he wanted to. Even though his first attempt to establish contact had been fruitless he couldn't back out now. He'd felt such an anti-climax when he'd found nobody at Leo Sharpe's address. Everything that had been bursting to the surface had to be stowed away again...at least for a little while longer.

He knelt there, still in his coat, for nearly half an hour before he picked up the phone and dialled.

\* \* \*

The images changed on the monitors but blackness still filled the office windows. Leo had little memory of the hours before or even after the drive from home. He could feel his head falling back. He closed his eyes and the buzz of the security booth faded as he drifted off. But when his head fell back further than was comfortable, he snapped awake. There was an image on his monitor and he blinked in disbelief at the familiar figure.

It was Laura staring up at him via the camera in the front car park. He'd seen her on the bank of security screens before – glimpses of her just leaving shot or polar impressions of her face that were there as he'd blinked awake. She'd once emerged from the shadows in the warehouse and told him that she wasn't in pain. The relief had quickly ebbed when he'd found himself in bed. But as he stretched his eyes sideways with his fingers and blinked them rapidly she still stared up at him.

It took a split second more for his brain to re-engage and then he realised it was Ashley, gesturing for him to let her in through the main doors. With the shadows overhead and her hair now a similar length to Laura's the likeness was unnerving.

He pushed the button and a buzzer sounded as she pulled on the handle. Moments later the door to his booth opened and in she came, bringing in some fresh air.

'Non-alcoholic bubbly.' She pulled the bottle out of a

glittery gift bag. 'Happy birthday,' she said with mock fatigue to rebut his bewildered expression.

He watched her remove her coat and the booth filled with her anise scent. She was wearing a coordinating grey roll neck and trousers. To Ashley, it was casual wear. 'My birthday was yesterday.'

'Nice try.' She looked round for a place to hang the coat and then threw it on the floor. 'Eighteenth of Feb?'

'Yes.'

'And today is the eighteenth...'

Why had he not considered that Matty had got it wrong? He'd rarely remembered Leo's birthday in the past. 'How come you're out so late?' he asked.

'It's not even ten. Any paper cups?' She moved behind and then kissed him, her lips brushing his cheek but her hands remaining on his shoulders. She pressed her cheek to the side of his head and held him there for a few moments before the pragmatic air returned. 'Don't say we'll have to share this...' She picked up his yellow coffee mug from the desk and appeared to be counting the rings inside.

He observed her as she pulled on the stack of water cones from the cooler in the corner of the booth. The same look of quiet determination pursed her lips and through pencilled eyebrows and lip-gloss that Laura never wore he could see the same infectious resolve in her profile.

*If she pulls off too many cups, we'll both see Laura
again.*

Two cones came away in her long, manicured nails.

Ashley popped the bubbly and poured a mouthful
into each cone. They tapped them together in a dull,
unspoken toast. It tasted like liver salts and they both
grimaced.

Ashley nodded, connoisseur-like, 'Interesting.'

Leo didn't drink because his father had done more
than enough for him and his brother put together. He'd
road-tested it plenty of times in the past year but had
been disappointed with the results. He'd anticipated
the loosening and warm embrace of oblivion that he'd
heard so much about but it had just made him sick.
Ashley had offered to tutor him but he'd already found
temazepam. She told him she'd rather get him drunk.

'Shame your birthday wasn't yesterday.'

'Why?'

'Bonsignore dying like that.' She deposited the cone
in the bin and used the action as an excuse not to meet
his eye. 'Has to be the best present of all.' But even
Ashley couldn't summon any conviction.

'I watched it with the Allan-Carlins. They've suddenly
decided that it's what they've been waiting for.'

Ashley didn't immediately seize on his comment.
'Perhaps that's what we need to believe as well.' She
tried to restrain him with a hazel stare.

Leo wanted to stand, to prove to himself that he

78

couldn't be caught unawares. 'Because he's dead and we can bury Laura with him?'

'No, because wherever Laura is the very last thing she'd want would be to see us unhappy.' She said it evenly.

'And that's now your decision as well?'

'No,' she sighed. 'But someone evil is dead and that should be some recompense.'

'Recompense enough?'

'Of course not.' She closed her eyes as if summoning inner reserves. 'But how many people have gone missing since Laura? Would that be justifiable if we just knew who had taken her? Bonsignore's confession—'

'Don't do this, Ash. Bonsignore said if he was going to be in jail for life it may as well be for something better than strangling his cunt boyfriend.'

Ashley's plea hardened. 'According to another inmate. You're prepared to believe the word of one inmate over another?'

'You know what the situation was before they leapt on his confession.'

'It's not me you have to convince about the convenience of his testimony, Leo. But you've got to start convincing yourself that Bonsignore's death can bring some balance.'

'It doesn't.' Leo felt the sudden, uncustomary volume of his words vibrate in his chest. He hadn't shouted but their solidity made Ashley blink. He felt a pang because he knew he was making it harder for her to do what she was asking of him.

'All we can do is believe what we want, Leo.'

'Bonsignore?'

'Bonsignore. Bookwalter...' She deliberately left the name hanging between them.

'But I don't believe Bookwalter.'

'Then why do you still entertain him?' Her tone was harsh now. She knew he'd be unable to keep his promise for the umpteenth time.

Leo tried to think of an appropriate answer but the delay was sufficient.

Anger prickled red above her cheekbones. 'Leo...' She struggled to keep it in check. 'For Laura's sake you can't go on associating with him.'

'I know what I'm doing.'

'Nonsense. You're vulnerable and that nut job knows it. How can you be so stupid?' She narrowed her eyes at him and he thought he was about to see the molten lava that Laura had often told him about.

'I won't let him manipulate me.'

'John Bookwalter is nothing but a parasite leeching off your grief. If you continue to give him control you'll never be able to move on.'

'Like everyone else is.' He knew he was deflecting.

Ashley bit her jaw. 'Nobody's forgetting Laura but you must promise not to speak to Bookwalter again... for her sake and mine.'

'All right,' he said evenly. But he stared at the monitors because he knew Ashley's expression would be as unconvinced as his reflection.

Later on, Leo was just heading for bed when he noticed the LED light of the answer machine flashing. There were three messages. He pressed the button to listen to them and got two hang-ups before a business-like, Indian voice filtered through the speaker.

'Mr Sharpe...this is Doctor...Mutatkar. I'm eager to speak to you and called at your home earlier this evening. I know where Laura is.'

# CHAPTER 10

'We must talk. Could you meet me tomorrow at 10pm in the Café Nero in Wick Street? It's only a few minutes from your house. Here is my mobile number.'

Leo wrote down the details and replayed the message. He still couldn't work out the caller's first name. It had been a while since he'd had a crank call. He supposed with the Vacation Killer back in the news some of the sickos who'd tracked down his number last year might still get a kick out of rekindling his despair.

He'd been flooded with them when Laura's name was all over the TV and many had made claims to have sighted her or known her location. Some had even pretended to be her. In desperation he'd agreed to meet two. One of them didn't show up and the other turned out to be a journalist.

It wasn't difficult for a person to track down his details. He'd found everything about himself on the internet, his home address, phone number, wedding photographs as well as details of his relationship with Laura that had been exchanged on websites and chatrooms populated by individuals with an obsessive interest in the Vacation Killer.

He listened to the message another four times. It was only an hour or so until the meeting but Leo doubted he could stay awake until then. The indentation of his mattress beckoned.

* * *

Having drunk four cups of coffee beforehand, Leo's latte in Café Nero remained untouched as he sat at a side counter and reminded himself why he hated being in public places. Every woman with her back to him was Laura, every man her kidnapper. He examined every face exposed to him and craned to see those that had their backs to him logic suspended while he projected her onto the most unlikely candidates. Her hair could have grown longer, been restyled, dyed or cut short and she could have gained or lost weight.

It was a torment that he rarely subjected himself to now and he knew that his solitary job had probably prevented him from going insane. However, the sensation of being under surveillance was something he couldn't shake. He'd certainly been followed during the initial investigation and he was convinced he was still being monitored. Leo would have felt utterly comfortable with it if he was a hundred per cent sure it was the police. The idea that his agony was being recorded and that this would one day vindicate him was one of his only comforts. The notion that it could be giving pleasure to the person who had begun it, however, was something he fought unsuccessfully to suppress.

He had to believe what Ashley believed, that they'd moved through a weird shutter in their lives but that it was now most definitely behind them. It had changed things irreversibly and made them both question the fabric of what was around them but Ashley was convinced that they had to move on before they were both left stranded. Fifteen months without a trace; Leo knew Ashley had slowly resigned herself to the fact that she would never see Laura again – he couldn't countenance this however, even though it was slowly eating him alive.

The door of the café swung inward and a rotund Indian man in a heavy blue woollen coat carrying a briefcase emerged through clouds of his own breath. Leo raised himself slightly from his stool to make his presence known but the man headed straight for the counter without looking around. Perhaps it wasn't him. Leo looked at his watch. 10.47. The man ordered a drink and then dumped himself at one of the lower couches facing the window. His head seemed to sink lower into his scarf as he sipped at his steaming coffee but he made no sign of interest in the other people around him.

'Doctor Mutatkar?' Leo found himself suddenly standing over the man.

The Indian man rolled his eyes up at Leo and shook his head once – quickly and in irritation. Without apologising Leo returned to his perch at the side counter.

He tried to visualise the person who had made the call and imagine where they were at that exact moment. At home, at work, watching him from across the street? Perhaps their prank had been forgotten the moment they'd put the phone down. He'd known what the outcome of the meeting would be but he still had no choice but to come.

It was the accent and the business-like tone of the message that had persuaded him that this one might be something more than a hoax. The ingenuous voice had definitely lacked the theatrical bait of other calls he'd received in the past. Leaving a phone number had also seemed unusually convincing. He was in the business of reading hope into every new and dirty crevice but it never ceased to amaze him how his situation continued to be a source of anonymous amusement for others.

He tried the number that he'd brought with him three times during the wait and got only an answering service. He tried one last time.

*If he answers now, he'll know where Laura is.*

He got the answering service again and decided to leave the coffee house. It was past eleven thirty. He stopped outside trying to catch the eye of anyone either side of the street but the human traffic bustled by in complete ignorance of him.

* * *

Doctor Mutatkar shifted in his car seat. There was no way he could have made the meeting. No way he could have shared his information with Leo Sharpe.

His neck had been snapped in the garage before he'd been deposited in the boot of his own car. He'd been driven round for a while, his chauffeur looking for an opening. There were a lot of cars and people around and it wasn't until they'd crawled to the end of the slip road that Doctor Mutatkar got to sit at the driving wheel for the last time.

His feet were positioned on the pedals and his head pressed back against the seat before the brake was released. The car was pushed back up the hill so it could gain enough momentum and then the engine was started.

As a healthy burst of traffic became visible through the thicket hiding the slip road, Doctor Mutatkar was released and rolled quickly down the hill .

The passenger window exploded first, showering his coat with cubic fragments of glass before the front of the lorry ploughed as far as the clinic pass keys that he kept in the ashtray. Then the weight and pressure of the lorry's wheel shattered rib bone and ground jagged spears into lungs and arteries. Mutatkar's internal organs were pulverised but it still had time to completely flatten the left side of his body before the impact spun the remains of the car and sent it scaling the wired rocks of the embankment. Eventually it came to rest on its side.

# CHAPTER 11

Even though he'd decided to wipe it Leo wanted to listen to Mutatkar's message one more time. But someone else had left a message since.

'Hey, Leo. How about heading over to us one day this week?' Matty said it as if it had just occurred to him and not like he'd been pursuing him for the past couple of months. 'You know where to reach us.'

*Us.* From misanthrope disappearing act to happy family plural in what felt like months. Leo wiped the message so only Mutatkar's remained and wondered why he continued to be so harsh on Matty. It had been months since his brother had moved in with Carla and the twins and he seemed to be making a real success of it. Did Leo resent Matty's ready-made family, particularly as it fell into place so soon after his own family plans had been suspended? Matty had been nothing but supportive since Laura's disappearance. Perhaps it was because he was still uncomfortable with his younger brother's newfound compassion. It was all a little too late in coming and it irked Leo that Matty had decided to start acting like a decent human being purely because he'd found his own happiness.

Matty had always been a non-presence in the most significant moments of Leo's life – a noticeable absence timed to generate maximum attention. He'd done it since they were kids and Matty had quickly learnt what a potent weapon not being there could be. Matty first vanished at Leo's sixth birthday party. It had only been for a few hours but it had shifted the focus of the guests away from the day's VIP and onto a frantic search for his younger brother. He'd been found playing quietly in the summerhouse – a location that had been scoured twice over.

Leo had suspected that Matty had simply snuck over the back wall of the garden and hidden there, ignoring the sound of his own name until the search had shifted to the front of the house. He'd then slipped back and stole into position, priming his look of baffled amusement for the relieved search party to discover him. At this stage the short winter afternoon had ebbed and it was time for the other guests to go home.

Even though the periods of his absence had got

longer, Matty always turned up. It was something that it seemed only Leo was wise to and he'd watched his parents, friends and Matty's potential girlfriends scurrying around in panic just moments after their attention had been focused a little too much in Leo's direction. How can somebody suddenly go missing? Indeed. Quite an enigma was Matty.

People didn't seem to question his absence as much when their parents fell ill, however. They'd been difficult times and Leo had spent them alone but there didn't seem to have been any great mystery about Matty's vanishing act then. Their mother had died of abdominal cancer in '95 and their father had quickly followed with liver cirrhosis the following year. Matty materialised in time for the funerals and everyone seemed as relieved to have him back as they had when they opened the summerhouse door. Eventual presence was the relief he gave to people. It was his gift.

Matty's last protracted absence had been the year of Leo's wedding. Leo hadn't wanted him as best man but, in the absence of an emigrated friend and against his better judgement, he had approached him to offer the role. Matty had seemed shocked to have been asked but accepted. Leo even thought that perhaps being given such a pivotal role would insure against the inevitable. It didn't, although Matty didn't disappear for the entire wedding day – just for the seven months leading up to it. It was his longest absence and for a while wedding plans had taken a back seat while Leo tried to locate him.

Matty appeared a day or so before and was actually present by the afternoon. He turned up customarily late for the civil ceremony but didn't actually vanish again until a few days later. On this occasion it was only a couple of weeks. Long enough, though, for Leo to spend his short married life again semi-concerned for his younger brother's safety. Then Laura vanished and, it seemed, stole Matty's thunder. He had reappeared after seeing her face on the news and Carla and the twins had kept him present ever since.

Leo would never know if Laura's disappearance had acted as an alarm call for Matty to settle down or an opportunity to have something his brother suddenly didn't: Leo loses wife and the prospect of having the family they had both planned for. At the same time Matty gets wife and two gorgeous children and is suddenly living in domestic nirvana. No, Matty had always sought attention but it had always been by removing himself rather than rubbing Leo's nose in anything. Leo suspected that it was his own suspended circumstances that made him so resentful.

He knew it wasn't a healthy train of thought but he just couldn't shake the notion that all the family-man business and brotherly concern was an act, with Matty performing in a way he only thought was expected. There was an emptiness in Matty and Leo sometimes wondered if only he saw it. Amongst the tight curls and awkwardness, a huge chunk of something was missing and it seemed, from a very young age, Matty could only fill it by taking from his brother.

* * *

*Ever heard of a Doctor Mutatkar?*

*Should I have?*

*He called me last night. Said he knew where Laura was. Was meant to meet me today but didn't show up.*

*I have a lot of devotees in the UK.*

*But you've never heard of him.*

*I didnt say that.*

*How much do you know of him then?*

*If he claims to know where Laura is then the question is how much does he know of me.*

Leo was exhausted and in no mood to disguise his impatience.

*Are you being deliberately cryptic or do you really not know him?*

Again, Bookwalter's answer immediately but sluggishly started to configure itself on the screen.

*Even locked away, ask him if he truly feels secure.*

Bookwalter could certainly think on his feet. It was the sort of abstruse statement that a good spiritualist would use. Like the ones that had been working for Maggie Allan-Carlin.

*How can I ask him anything? I told you – he didn't show up.*

*My mistake. Ask him the next chance you get.*

Leo tried to remember if he'd just got back from a shift or was due to start one. Whatever side of the sleep partition he was he had less patience for Bookwalter's arch responses.

*Is Laura with you?*

*Nearby.*

*Meant to ask. Has she made you any of her famous prawn toast yet?*

*Not a fan of oriental cuisine.*

It was a typical response because Bookwalter knew exactly what Leo was doing. Leo wondered if he'd use the titbit in a future exchange but doubted it. He'd deliberately forced incongruous information into their exchanges in the past but Bookwalter was meticulous and used only information that he'd insidiously extracted from Leo in his portfolio. Laura was allergic to sesame seeds but chances were Bookwalter would now steer clear of anything related to the subject.

He now implemented very little Leo gave him and usually adhered to his own (often incorrect) profile of Laura. When Leo had pulled him up on inaccuracies in the past, however, Bookwalter countered by using Laura's fictional presence to chide Leo for not knowing her well enough. There was only one time Bookwalter

94

had quoted Laura directly. It had been during a conversation about her love of theatre, which had been news to Leo. On that occasion, the words were so patently not hers and Bookwalter had let his own American diction filter through.

*She says I'm so mad you forgot that about me.*

Bookwalter never did it again and direct interaction with Laura had been forbidden ever since.

*Do I need to be concerned about Mutatkar?*

As usual, there was no period of reflection before Bookwalter answered.

*No.*

Ashley was right. Why the hell did he still entertain him? Was it because he was the only person left who was willing to talk about Laura as if she was still alive? Partly. More important than that, a man who had never set foot in the United Kingdom, let alone Chevalier's, was the only individual who had significantly projected what had happened the day Laura vanished.

Leo registered the blackness around the edges of his navy bedroom curtains and returned his attention to his laptop.

*Tell me again about the 12th.*

*Theres nothing more to add.*

But Leo knew that there would be and that Bookwalter's fingers would already be poised.

*Do you realise that of the thousands of people who visit my site youre the only person to ask about the mechanics of my abduction of Laura. In fact most of the questions Ive had to fence from others in relation to her seems to be whether she was my victim at all*

*They're all ghouls. They're not interested because you imply that she's still alive.*

*But only you and I know that for sure.*

*No – only you know that for sure. And Laura, of course.*

*Of course but thats because you continually deny yourself the opportunity to remove all doubt.*

*If you allowed me to speak directly to Laura then you would immediately remove all doubt.*

Although Leo had never caused Bookwalter to display any anger within his dialogue he knew when he was entering the sort of territory that might cut their discourse short. It was the fundamental weakness of Bookwalter's claim that often led to a terse suspension of their discussions. Whether Laura was his willing prisoner or there under duress – something that Bookwalter would never confirm one way or the other – Laura's real presence was something that could be confirmed in seconds and it was these definitive questions that Bookwalter was aggravated by and continually evaded.

Leo thought he was past deriding his lies but the

96

ludicrous pretence upon which their exchanges was based was sometimes so conspicuous that Leo had to fight his own reflex to attack him. He was either a delusional egocentric, a professional fraud who recognised the virtues of his grossly inflated claims attracting advertisers to his site – or both. However, Bookwalter's theories masquerading as accounts of his exploits were actually the closest thing Leo had to a plausible explanation for Laura's disappearance, and their convincing rationale meant he had to suppress a constant urge to needle him. A continually refined narrative had been emerging over months of mutual indulgence, and as Leo helped him fill in the gaps it became more credible than anything the police had speculated.

*Why is it that nobody but you cares for the fate of Laura Sharpe? Ive murdered many people, more than Bonsignore confessed to after he throttled his boyfriend and took the credit for my work.*

This was the point at which Leo held the punch bag. He'd never asked Bookwalter why he'd murdered the people he declared to have. His claim to be holding Laura was the only focus of their dialogue and he often wondered if that rankled with him. Bookwalter was a crank and a liar and Leo felt no need to grill him about crimes he hadn't committed. It also seemed bad taste to ask why he no longer killed because he knew Bookwalter's well-documented disgust for his media coverage was such a convenient excuse for suspending his activities. Leo did, however, genuinely wonder who he was. Had he dispensed with his real life wholesale in favour of his fictional persona and warped celebrity? There was very little on the internet that Bookwalter hadn't generated himself. News reports had simply described him as an 'out of work actor with an unhealthy fixation for serial killers.'

He'd never been remotely aggressive towards Leo but he often wondered if this was more to do with the fact Bookwalter was keen to nurture their relationship for financial gain. He'd watched a few of his grainy home-shot rants on YouTube – in fact, Bookwalter had once embedded all of them onto his own site – and all of them had revolved around his dissatisfaction with his media perception which he laid squarely at the feet of Bonsignore. The venom directed from one proven liar to another potential fraud was either the ultimate illustration of his performance skills or an indication as to how completely unhinged he was.

*Why have you now stopped attacking Bonsignore on the site?*

Leo tried to improve Bookwalter's mood by accommodating him so he could gear the conversation back to Chevalier's.

*Bonsignore was an amateur but Ive been dealing with second hand charlatans since I began. I now understand the trick is not to give them oxygen.*

98

*But if they're claiming to be responsible for acts they couldn't possibly have committed surely they can be immediately dismissed?*

Leo guessed the comment wouldn't have the resonance with Bookwalter that he intended.

There was only a brief pause before he responded.

*Not if people are determined to believe them.*

Leo doubted he was responding to his barb and thought it far more likely that Bookwalter was still caught up in his own mortification.

*So you think people don't care about the truth if their desperation can be satisfied?*

*Exactly. Its why you puzzle me, Leo. If you care so much for your own wife why have you never accepted my offer of hospitality?*

# CHAPTER 12

Leo wondered if Bookwalter's repeated offer to pay for a flight to New Orleans was as carefully calculated as he believed it was. As far as he knew, none of the other victims' families had had anything to do with Bookwalter. Any association beyond Leo and Bookwalter's dialogues was sure to be shamelessly capitalised upon.

*Send me the answers I want and I'll book a flight tomorrow.*

There were times Leo couldn't help himself. There was an exact degree of belief suspension that was required to maintain the attention of Bookwalter's skewed intellect and Leo wondered if he'd overstepped the mark. Leo had sent a list of intimate questions that only he and Laura would know the answers to during their initial dialogues and Bookwalter gave the same response every time Leo highlighted the fact that they had never been answered.

> *Laura wants you to come find her. Removing all doubt by answering those questions would be too easy.*

> *I need you to help me understand why Laura would want to test me in that way.*

> *If these exchanges are the limit of your concern for her safety then its understandable that Laura has mislaid her affection for you.*

> *You still forbid direct contact or to allow us to talk through you. You won't even tell me what the state of her health is or whether you've harmed her. Surely you can understand why I'm still sceptical.*

> *Its not my job to convince you, Leo. Ive told you where she is. Whether you choose to act upon it is your choice.*

Leo resisted the urge to go over the same ground with Bookwalter but found his fingers typing a question he'd asked him numerous times in the past.

> *So why didn't you murder her?*

> *For the same reason I had to murder the others.*

This other stock response was word for word the same as the other times but it was Ashley's disapproval that Leo visualised as he typed in the inevitable.

> *Because the email came back to you?*

Whether Bookwalter was deranged enough to believe he was the Vacation Killer and was holding Laura captive or was completely sane, he had to know that it was one question Leo needed to know the answer to.

*Because the email came back to me.*

This was why Leo still entertained Bookwalter. Even though he'd put the words at his disposal Bookwalter continually repeated what he yearned to be told.

* * *

*You were telling me about the 12th. What else can you remember?*

Leo felt his legs going to sleep but didn't uncross them from under the laptop.

*That a casual air makes you invisible. You both walked past me when you were looking for your usual table in Chevaliers. I passed you in the stairwell leading to the upstairs seating area.*

*How long had you been there?*

*A minute or so before you arrived. Id walked into the downstairs lounge but nobody was tending bar. It had only just opened so I walked the length of the place to see if Laura had come in. She was always very punctual particularly with Opallios being just across the street. There werent any other customers when I walked to the upstairs bar. She wasnt at her usual table so I came back down the stairs and thats when you guys were coming the other way.*

*I don't remember seeing you there.*

Fact was, Leo couldn't remember whether he had seen anyone or not. Their arrival at Chevalier's was a weekly event so one visit mirrored the others. It was usually early lunchtime when they entered which meant they had their pick of the tables but he couldn't recall if it had been completely empty or if there'd been a smattering of other customers settling in. It just hadn't registered because they'd been talking and had made a beeline for their usual location. His brain must have dispensed with the memory before they'd even sat down but Leo would have given anything to recall the thirty-yard walk to the place where he had last seen Laura.

*I dont remember what you wore, Leo. Laura had that mustard knitted top on so she seemed dressed differently to normal.*

*How would she normally dress?*

*Not as informally. She let her hair down with Hektor the other times Id watched her having lunch there but she was usually dressed for work. She looked really tall close up. It was quite a surprise and I remember wondering if she would fit in the trunk of the car. I turned back in your direction as you both climbed the stairs and realised that it was all down to the heels she was wearing. It all worked out though. I had no reason to remove them.*

*Where did you go then?*

*As a reflex, into the restroom and then into one of the cubicles. Didnt lock the door, just closed it nearly all the way and lifted my feet off the tiles. Nobody came in though. I wondered if either of you had seen me. I doubted it. You were both engrossed with each other.*

*What were we talking about?*

*Christmas shopping from what I could understand.*

Leo had no recollection of what they'd been talking about or, indeed, if they'd been talking at all when they headed for their usual leather sofa.

*I decided you hadnt seen me but that I could still back myself up if you had.*

*With the story about the broken statue?*

*Correct. Thats when I came back out of the restroom and found her pushing the door to the ladies. I knew everything would fall into place after that.*

*So you had second thoughts beforehand?*

*Happens all the time. You watch and learn but the skill is in recognising the opportunity. Do the names Libby Morgan, Julie Desouza or Martin Cornish mean anything to you?*

*No.*

*That's because they shouldnt. Right now theyre probably enjoying lives I very nearly took from them. My research was thorough but the right occasion never presented itself. You can plan for every eventuality but you still need luck. When I met Laura in that confined space and she made eye contact I knew wed walk out of that place like we were invisible.*

This was new insight that Bookwalter had never embroidered the story with before.

*The first thing I say is her name. It always disarms people because they think they should know you. Theyre offguard while they try to find you in their head and in those few seconds you can do anything. Then shes looking at my delivery guy uniform and Im laughing and going out of my way to put her at her ease. I throw in Opallios and the name of her boss and tell her I've been sent over to the bar because they figured shed be there. Ive got a parcel for her to sign for and I'm holding up the digital signature display but before she can process this Im telling her that I think its a statue and that it sounds like its probably broken.*

Leo noticed that on each occasion Bookwalter immersed himself in his own story the past tense suddenly became the present. His typing got faster and his mistakes became more frequent, his frantic and categorical corrections prompting Leo to imagine him punching the keys and cursing himself as they interrupted the flow of his account.

*Ive given her so much thats familiar to her. Im wearing the uniform, Im holding the signature display for her to sign and I say Ive been trying to find her. I say Im illegally parked in Percy Street and can she come get the parcel before I get a ticket.*

*Im overloading her with information and at that point her eyes go up and to the right – up the stairs to where youre waiting. It's the crucial moment. I tell her that it's not a very big parcel and could she come get it now because I dont want another parking ticket for Christmas. Thats when her eyes drop again. Maybe she feels sorry for me, maybe she digs my American accent, maybe she doesnt want to go back up the stairs in those heels again and figures it will be easier just to come get it. Add to that the fact that her mystery Christmas parcel is already damaged. She tells me she just needs to use the bathroom and I tell her Ill wait.*

*I lean against the wall at the bottom of the stairs and youre waiting for her at the top of them. If you come down I can just walk out. If anyone passes me and takes note of me I can just walk out. I know neither of these*

106

*things will happen though and all I have to do is look harassed when Laura comes back out of the restrooms and hope she hasnt thought too hard about anything. Not that there was anything wrong with my story but sometimes common sense can slow the impetus.*

*Shes back out in under a minute though and she obviously peed as fast as she could. Shes considered telling you whats going on but shes decided against it particularly now shes held me up further by answering the call of nature. I walk her quickly out of Chevaliers and she has to keep up. Theres still nobody in the front bar and I hold the door open for her.*

Leo's mouth was dry. He sipped at his coffee and it was stone cold.

*Percy Street is a block up from Chevaliers on the right. I pretend to be programming the digital signature display with a touch pen and dont make eye contact. We turn the corner into Percy Street and walk down the right hand sidewalk. I keep my head down but peer up through my eyebrows for pedestrians. There are three kids standing on the opposite side of the street but theyre not looking at us. Laura says something but I dont hear what it is.*

*I fix the kids until were masked by the row of cars parked down the sidewalk. The street is a dead end and I turn off the display and ask Laura to sign. She tells me its turned itself off and I pretend to be fixing it as we approach the dead end. I hand it back to her and know that in the time it takes her to sign my story will have run out. Ive left the trunk of the car unlocked and Ive got the hypodermic in her left side while her hands are still busy. I neck lock her and push my knuckles into her mouth until I feel her shoulders sag. I take my time putting her into the boot of the car because I know nobody will disturb us.*

107

The cursor flashed. Bookwalter seemed to be waiting for a prompt. Either that or he just wanted to know that Leo was still there.

*Percy Street is overlooked on the right hand side by several housing blocks. Weren't you concerned that somebody would have seen you?*

Percy Street had nothing but horded wasteland bordering it at the time of Laura's disappearance.

*I told you, I knew nobody would disturb us. I used the plastic carpet ties on her wrists but I didnt bother with her feet. The tranquilliser would still be working hours after wed reached our destination. Then something happened just before I shut the trunk.*

*I remember you telling me.*

But Leo knew that Bookwalter's elaborations were always building to this moment. It was the most convincing part of the account and no matter what additional facts he embellished the story with as he gleaned more specific details from Leo, Bookwalter's narrative always concluded with the same recollection.

*I dont know whether it was a reflex or if it was Laura being guileful as she went under but when I checked the ties on her wrists she curled her fingers around the tops of mine. She didnt grab them, she seemed to caress the three fingers of my right hand and I remember how it had taken me out of the moment.*

*Id held her while the tranquilliser had taken effect, had her teeth marks in the back of my hand and had lifted her weight into the trunk but that was the first time shed*

108

*touched me. It definitely unnerved me and I remember slapping her hand away and slamming the boot.*

Leo waited for Bookwalter to continue. The account always ended here but he wondered if he was going to polish the final memory more than he usually did. Memory? The whole account was a fantasy that Bookwalter got off on but he wasn't sure if he reverted back to the past tense as a natural way to end his story or because the detail about the fingers was part of a genuine recollection. The moment seemed utterly convincing to Leo but Bookwalter had proved himself to be an adroit storyteller. He employed convincingly odd details, had garnered small pieces of truth from Leo in the past and used them to plug the holes in the places he couldn't have been.

In his initial outline of events Bookwalter told Leo he'd watched them sitting at their table through the window of Chevalier's. The table had been in the back lounge where there was no window. He'd also told Leo that he'd seen Laura in Chevalier's most lunchtimes. She mostly ate at her desk at Opallios and Leo usually accompanied her whenever she did drink there. He still also maintained that there were toilets at the bottom of the stairs leading down from the back lounge. There were no stairs, only one single step and no toilets. The stairs actually led up from the front bar to the central lounge where there were toilets halfway along the right-hand wall.

He could certainly pinpoint the origins of all the other information that Bookwalter had about Opallios and Hektor from their many dialogues. The other details, like the description of what Laura had been wearing, would have been available to Bookwalter through news broadcasts and on the internet.

He continually asked Bookwalter where he'd taken Laura from there but had been told that details of what transpired afterwards would be too 'taxing'. For Leo or Bookwalter? There was, of course, the small matter of how he'd managed to transplant her to the United States against her will. Bookwalter occasionally insinuated that Laura was now a willing accomplice but how had he got himself present at Chevalier's when he'd never left the state of Louisiana in his entire life?

They were questions that all had one definitive answer. But even dispensing with the inconsistencies in Bookwalter's own ludicrous claims the delivery guy story was still the most convincing theory that Leo had been offered in fifteen months of personal and police investigation. He'd even started to see Bookwalter the delivery guy in his dreams and waking to the knowledge that his delusional correspondent had deliberately planted himself there never completely shook the notion that Bookwalter had become one of the last people in his life who confirmed that Laura existed.

*Have to go to sleep now. Say good night to Laura for me.*

Leo didn't wait for a response but shut the lid of his laptop and lay back on the pillows. He thought about taking off his uniform but turned off the lamp instead and scrabbled for the water and pills. He was asleep before he found them.

# CHAPTER 13

As the light in Leo's room went out Cleaves was just trimming his fingernails. The clippings pinged off the condensation on the windscreen and he turned the warm air on to clear it. Another freezing morning. Night-time vigils were fine but the street was about to get busy and he'd have to move the car every half hour so nobody would alert the police.

The car had nearly ended up as a write-off but that had been Sharpe's stupid fault. He ran his hand over his head again and felt the sharp prickles of his recent haircut. At least there was no shortage of nearby shops to keep him feeling human. He flipped the sun visor down so he could study the grey hairs amongst the black. He wondered if he should try a spray dye. Perhaps he'd wait for his bald patch to spread a little more first. It wouldn't be long and the thought made his stomach shrink. His wife had told him she didn't mind but he was only in his mid thirties. He kept his abs trim but what the fuck was the point if his follicles were heading towards premature middle age?

His phone rang and he switched his earpiece on. There was only one person it was allowed to be while he was working.

'Progress?' Cleaves could hear the motor of a train in the background. His employer was obviously on his way to work.

'Nothing significant.' He'd been reporting the same thing since he'd taken on the job and had reached the point when he'd run out of different ways to say it.

'I'll call you in a couple of days' time.' He hung up.

Cleaves turned off his earpiece. That was another three days expenses then. What the fuck, it was Mr Allan-Carlin's money.

* * *

When the phone rang Leo reached for the bedside table but found that he was sitting in the security booth. He extended his other arm and picked up, vaguely registering that it was morning through the windows on the multiscreens in front of him.

'Leo?'

'Ashley?' Whatever the time, it was definitely too early in the morning to be hearing from her.

'I couldn't sleep,' she said by way of explanation. 'Sat

114

watching reruns of *Frasier*. Seems to be on twenty-four hours a day.'

'I was just...' Leo tried to think about what he was just doing but his sentence tailed off.

He heard the volume of the TV drop and the sound of Ashley laying the remote onto a hard surface. 'What was the name of the doctor who left a message on your answering machine?'

For a moment Leo had forgotten that he'd mentioned it to her in a phone call. He was convinced that he'd never remember the doctor's name but found it rolling effortlessly off his tongue. 'Mutatkar.'

'Right. I was flicking round and caught the headlines on News 24. I knew I'd heard the name and I've only just realised why. Somebody called Mutatkar's committed suicide.'

Leo felt something coil up inside him. 'When?'

'Couple of days ago. Wasn't headline material until now though. Hang on, the paper's already arrived. Let me see if there's anything about it in there.'

Leo watched the cleaners arriving on the screens in front of him and listened to rustling paper on the other end of the line.

'Here it is.' Leo visualised Ashley putting her spectacles on. 'Police believed eminent physician, Doctor Parag Mutatkar, committed suicide by driving into the pathway of an oncoming goods lorry on the afternoon of March 12th. However subsequent examination suggests that the fifty-five-year-old was dead before the accident occurred. A full autopsy is now being undertaken.'

The line seemed to go dead. 'Ash?'

'That's all.'

'Is there a photo?' Leo wasn't sure why he'd asked. He'd never seen the man and no matter how many times he'd replayed the message he still hadn't been able to discern the name as Parag.

'Yes. Nothing else though. Bizarre story.'

'Which paper?'

'The *Telegraph*. Wait a minute. Should I really have told you this?' She suddenly sounded full of self-reproach. 'Remember, it's probably a complete coincidence.'

* * *

Dr Parag Mutatkar MB BS FRCP MRCS DCH DRCOG wasn't hard to find. An eminent rheumatologist who had owned his own clinic in Notting Hill, he had been Council and Executive member of the British Society for Rheumatology, an expert adviser to NICE, scientific adviser to the National Osteoporosis Society, and honorary treasurer to the Arthritis and Musculoskeletal Alliance. He was one day away from his fifty-sixth birthday when the lorry had ploughed into his car. He left behind a wife, Dakini, and a twenty-two-year-old daughter, Sabri.

Could he really be the same Doctor Mutatkar and, if so, what the hell had he been doing leaving messages on Leo's answering machine?

116

Leo had wondered if he would be ex-directory but a quick scan through the Kensington and Chelsea online phone book had pinpointed the sprawling Queen Anne house that Leo's Saab was now parked outside. He'd wondered if there'd be a mob of reporters outside the black electric gates when he arrived but the story obviously hadn't been worth a wait in the cold or was already old news.

He got out of the car, crossed the road and pushed on the intercom buzzer beside the gate.

*If somebody answers in five seconds then this will be my first real step towards finding Laura.*

Nobody did and as he looked up the gravel driveway to the house again he noticed that some of the windows still had their curtains drawn.

'Hello.' The female Indian voice sounded faint.

'Hello. Mrs Mutatkar?'

'No, that's my mum.'

Leo could hear another voice behind the first.

'Who is this?' The second female Indian voice had extra layers of weary maturity.

'I'm sorry to disturb you at a time like this.'

'Are you from the papers?'

'No. I may have known your husband. No, that's not true. Your husband may have telephoned me a few days ago.'

Leo could hear her breathing for a few moments. 'Nice try, but please leave us alone.'

'Mrs Mutatkar, please believe me. I'm as surprised to find myself knocking at your door as you are but there is one way of confirming this without even letting me onto your property.'

He heard her sigh. 'We just want to be left alone.'

'And I promise I will leave you be once we've had a chance to talk. My name is Leo Sharpe. My wife was kidnapped in 2007 and a couple of nights ago a Doctor Mutatkar left a message on my answering machine saying that he knew where she was.'

Another pause. 'Sorry, what is this all about?'

'He asked me to meet him the following morning and left his mobile number. Can you confirm that his number is...' Leo plucked the piece of paper out of his pocket that he'd scribbled the number on and recited it to her.

'Anybody could have that information.'

Leo's circulation surged. So it was him. It was the an interesting development and suddenly he felt a new impetus brushing his awkwardness aside. He leant further in to the intercom as if she would be able to hear the truth in the volume of his words. 'I tried to meet him...he said at 10 o'clock in Wick Street, Wednesday morning...' He gave her time to absorb the information and an opportunity to remember the day in question. 'When he didn't turn up, I called him on the number he gave me. If you look in his phone there should be a record of a missed call from my number.'

'Wait a moment.' Her voice became incoherent but he could tell from the tone that she was issuing an instruction away from the intercom. He shivered but he wasn't sure if it was the cold.

After a rustling that Leo couldn't identify. 'What is your number?' She sounded more suspicious.

He told her.

Another pause. 'How did you say you know my husband?'

'That's just it, I don't.'

'According to this phone, you were the last person to call him.'

The gate buzzed and then opened.

# CHAPTER 14

Leo crunched up the driveway and the front door opened against the chain. He could just make out the diminutive figure of Mrs Mutatkar standing beyond the crack.

'Why have you not gone to the police?' she asked warily.

'Because I've had over a year's experience of their incompetence.'

'Did you say your wife is...missing?'

'Your husband told me he knew where she was.' He sensed her nervousness. 'I could go to the police with this.'

He saw Mrs Mutatkar blink and then the door closed. For a moment he stood on the step wondering if that was it but then the chain rattled. She'd obviously thought about leaving him out there but Leo sensed something else in her behaviour besides antipathy towards an unwanted caller. He'd thought mentioning the police had been a hollow bluff but it had more of an obvious effect that he'd anticipated.

The door opened wide to reveal a barefoot Mrs Mutatkar clad in a cerise silk, ankle-length dressing gown. She was smaller than she'd looked through the crack and had the sort of complexion that belied her age. How old was she? Probably in her mid-to-late fifties but the only giveaway was how sunken her eyes were. He wondered if that had been the result of the past few days, because apart from her dark bob of hair looking slightly tousled, Mrs Mutatkar was immaculate. He saw her daughter, much taller than her and wearing a long T-shirt, leaning nervously against the breakfast bar in the kitchen at the end of the hallway.

'So sorry to intrude on your grief.' Having barged into her home it seemed a ridiculous thing to say.

'Come through,' Mrs Mutatkar whispered, then turned her back on him and padded through the thick-carpeted hallway towards the kitchen.

Leo followed and took in the interior, especially the portraits of the family trio on the walls. Doctor Mutatkar smiled out of a photo that, judging from the age of his daughter, looked to have been taken recently. Outwardly, everything seemed to indicate a happy and successful family.

'Sabri, make us some tea.'

Mrs Mutatkar's daughter was beautiful. She flicked her long ponytail, placed the transparent polythene bag that she was holding on the breakfast bar and went to the kettle at the far end of the long, modern kitchen. Leo took in the contents of the bag. It contained a wallet, some keys, a selection of plastic security swipe cards and some pens.

'We weren't meant to open it. The police want his personal effects returned but his phone was in it.' Mrs Mutatkar placed her fingers gently on the bag and seemed lost for words.

Leo felt himself start to apologise again but stopped himself. 'No tea for me thanks. I don't want to encroach on your time. It's just I can't begin to understand why your husband would have claimed to know where my wife is.'

'My husband is a brilliant man.' She paused, aware that the statement should have been past tense. 'He made me – us – most proud.'

Sabri finished filling the kettle and clicked the lid on.

'No tea, Sabri. Wait for me in the lounge.'

Doctor Mutatkar's daughter walked past them casting them both a wary eye. Leo noticed that her features had more maturity than he'd first thought.

Mrs Mutatkar waited until she was out of earshot. 'Tell me about your wife.'

Leo told Mrs Mutatkar about Laura and while he listened to his own story she pulled her dressing gown tighter to her neck and looked in any direction but his.

His lips shaped the familiar words and dates and places but this time they didn't prompt the dry sickness he always felt when he articulated them for the thousandth time over.

Mrs Mutatkar scraped out a stool and sat down heavily. She sighed and pinched the bridge of her nose as if relieving pressure until he'd finished. 'I know nothing of this or why my husband would have phoned you – believe me.' She looked at Leo and he could see the pain in the dark recesses of her eyes. 'There are no answers for you here – from us – I promise.' She arranged the tie of her dressing gown in her lap but she knew he was waiting for her to continue. 'You won't go to the police?' It was more a plea than a condition.

'I'm tired of the police...but I'll do anything that's necessary to find Laura and if that means they have to become involved...'

Mrs Mutatkar held up her hand. She closed her eyes and her lips twisted as if she were flinching from a wound. 'Parag always provided for us. But sometimes people...people aren't completely who you think they are. I found that out at the end of last summer.' She looked at the doorway as if expecting to find her daughter listening there. 'I know as much as I want

124

to...which is very little. Soon, though, I think I may have to know more.'

Leo felt something inflating at the base of his throat.

She inhaled some composure. 'Post these back to me when you've finished. I don't want you to call here again.' She leant sideways and pulled open a drawer. She produced a key ring and placed it on the bar with the flat of her hand, her gold rings scraping against its metal as she slid it towards Leo. 'They're for a room in Camden Town, 17 Bell Terrace. Do you need me to write it down?'

Leo shook his head but she didn't meet his gaze.

Mrs Mutatkar seemed to deflate now she'd given him the keys. 'I went to the terrace once. I found the keys and one evening I followed Parag there when I knew he'd taken them with him.' She seemed suddenly breathless. 'It was the place he went when he wasn't a husband or father. I've been trying to pretend that it doesn't exist.' Mrs Mutatkar closed the drawer with the heel of her hand. 'If there are any answers they can only be there. If they're not, I can't help you further.' She looked back in the direction her daughter had left.

* * *

Number 17 Bell Terrace was the last sort of place that Leo expected. It was in a respectable enough residential street and the key allowed him access to

125

a well-maintained Victorian house crouching behind two topiary cone privets via a yellow front door. He found himself in a bright and airy hallway where the smell of carpet shampoo vied with nicotine. The walls and doors were painted fresh white and there was the sound of a TV coming from the end. The second key had the number 4 scratched into the green rubber grip end.

He climbed the carpeted staircase to his left which took him to a darkened landing that smelt of yesterday's roast dinner. From behind Door 1 which was directly in front of him, he could hear the sound of a TV. The door to his left was a communal bathroom, still steaming from somebody's recent use. Leo gripped the wooden banister and followed the rail past doors 2 and 3 until he came to the last one. He paused outside and listened for sounds of movement from within.

Suddenly, the sound of the TV got louder and he turned to find an overweight woman, with her hair wrapped in a towel, emerging from room 1. She cast him a cursory glance but seemed to think nothing of his presence there. She went into the bathroom, shutting the door behind her. Leo returned his attention to the door and inhaled, suddenly realising that his sense of smell seemed suddenly acute. He wondered what time it was; he would normally be submerged in temazepam oblivion by now.

*If the key turns easily, Laura is getting nearer.*

It did, and the door cracked as it opened, as if it had recently been painted. Leo pushed the door wide, bumping it against an armchair that sat behind the door. He took in the room. With its single bed covered by a handmade quilt cover, it was hardly a mistress flat. There was a thick scent in there, like josssticks. The room was as brightly painted as the rest of the house and furnished with the sort of motley collection of old furniture that you'd expect to find in a bedsit.

The curtains were shut but the bright daylight filtered in through the thin yellow material. He walked inside and glanced in every corner – not knowing who or what he expected to see. He closed the door and walked to the window, pulling open the curtains and peering through the nets. He was looking down on the small front garden and the tops of the topiary trees.

Leo sat in the armchair that was positioned in the bay window and scrutinised the low table beside him. It contained a stack of different sized dinner plates, a cutlery holder, toaster and a slightly rusting tray that held teacups, a kettle and a pot. In front of him was a fridge with a microwave sitting on top and beyond that a wardrobe. He rose again and opened the door. He found one casual blue jacket hanging up and a pair of black leather shoes. He checked the pockets of the jacket and found a spare button in a cellophane packet.

As he opened and shut the drawers of the dirty white dressing table on the opposite side of the single bed there appeared to be little sign of Doctor Mutatkar's occupation of the room bar a few rattling pens and a box of matches. When, as an afterthought, he pulled the slim drawer beneath the mirror, however, it refused to budge. There was a hole for a smaller key on the front but he didn't need to look at the keys Mrs Mutatkar had given him to know neither of them was small enough to fit.

He fetched a knife from the cutlery drawer and tried to prise it. He managed to get the edge of the blade into the gap but the knife bent at the handle as he levered it. He tried another. It wasn't a sturdy drawer but the lock was obviously solid and the second knife warped with his exertion as well. He took a step back and aimed the side of his heel once at the drawer before kicking it. It didn't budge but a chunk of the ornate wood on the corner had chipped off so he kicked it again.

The front of the drawer cracked and he waited, listening to his uneven breathing, to see if anyone would come to investigate the noise. When nobody did, he stabbed the crack of the drawer with one of the knife handles until the front caved in. He let his knees take his weight and peered into the frontless drawer. There were a number of objects within the darkened recess but he only needed to remove the first to know what the others were.

It was a small glass pipe with a small bowl that

was burnt on the outside. There was some dark residue within it. Leo sat cross-legged on the carpet and fished out a few of the foil-wrapped twists and packets and dropped them between his legs. That the doctor had been a crack addict was unexpected but Leo felt around in the drawer for something more. When his knuckles butted the end of the drawer he withdrew his hand.

Dejected, he hoisted himself to his feet again and looked around the room, his gaze coming to rest on the bed. An MP3 player lay on the bedside table and he could picture Doctor Mutatkar sprawled out insensibly with it attached to his ears, time and respectability frozen for however many hours he spent here. Then he noticed the laptop. Resting on its edge, its slim grey casing scarcely noticeable against the frowzy white cover sheet. A phone line trailed from it into the socket beside the bed.

Leo sat cross-legged in the middle of the bed and lifted it onto the counterpane. He flapped the lid open and switched it on. As the laptop buzzed to life, he heard himself dry swallow and felt the familiar prickling in the tops of his shoulders.

*If it asks me for a password, Laura has to be hidden here somewhere.*

No password was requested and the desktop suddenly cluttered itself with named files. However, he instinctively clicked on the email icon. The inbox had been scrupulously emptied but received thirteen new messages. None were personal and they all appeared to be block update emails from medical organisations. He closed it and focused on the desktop, clicking on one folder at random.

Several documents were saved inside and Leo opened the first and scrolled through it quickly. It outlined the detailed findings of a drug trial and its effect on arthritis patients. Obviously the doctor wasn't averse to mixing business with pleasure. Leo closed it and opened another, working his way from top to bottom through the remaining files on the desktop and finding dozens of documents inside each one before opening the My Documents folder. It was crammed with hundreds more. This was going to take hours to work through and Leo considered unplugging the laptop and taking it home.

He looked up from the screen and round the room and again tried to visualise Doctor Mutatkar whiling away hour upon hour shut away from his family and colleagues. Then he remembered what Bookwalter had said when he'd asked him about Mutatkar:

*Even locked away, ask him if he truly feels secure.*

Leo shut the documents window and opened the doctor's email again.

# CHAPTER 15

*Wouldnt the good doctor be alarmed to know youre using his laptop?*

Leo hadn't been surprised to find Bookwalter online. He rarely wasn't and the website and its maintenance appeared to be his full-time occupation. He'd already told him whose laptop he was logging in from.

*He's finished with it.*

*????*

Leo wondered if Bookwalter really knew anything of the doctor's death and had already decided to keep the information he conveyed to a minimum.

*What did you mean about him being locked away?*

*We all like to feel impregnable.*

Another recondite response. As always, Bookwalter could know everything or nothing. He was about to attempt to solicit something more specific when Bookwalter added a footnote.

*Do you feel impregnable?*

*How about giving me something to convince me you know as much as you give the impression you do.*

*Not my job. Just like acting as a go-between for you and Laura isnt. You want to speak to her you come see me. Now is a good time, vacation season hasnt started yet.*

*Do you think the Doctor would be interested in tagging along?*

*All are welcome though some may be more high maintenance guests than others.*

Again, the words rattled out slowly with no pause for thought and again Bookwalter managed to imbue his response with the right measure of grainy, subjective relevance.

*How do you think Laura would react to a visit from Mutatkar?*

*I cant speak for her because shes indisposed but I would guess shed be as surprised to see him as she would you.*

*Then maybe we'll both consider making the trip.*

It was easy enough when he was alone at home but sitting in a dead stranger's room using a dead stranger's laptop seemed to remove any last anchors of his own reality.

*Just give me the word and I can make all the arrangements. Remember, Ill cover the whole trip out here.*

*Let me consult with Doctor Mutatkar when I see him later and I will give you his response.*

*Id like to believe youre not putting me on.*

*Why ever would you think I was doing that?*

*Because Laura would be so disappointed if you were. Can I take it that I can go tell her the good news?*

*Of course.*

*Great. What date can I tell her?*

For the first time Leo saw how he could completely let go of his reality and indulge in the fantasy as much as Bookwalter did.

*Will discuss with Doctor Mutatkar. Do you have a message for him?*

*More a belated piece of advice for you both. Dont leave without saying goodbye. You might never get the chance again.*

\* \* \*

6.05

Leo glanced at the clock in his living room and thought about food for the first time. Less than two hours until he was on duty. Mutatkar's confiscated laptop had so absorbed him that time had sped by, hours sneakily speeding outside the closed blinds while he scanned every conceivable folder. The phone rang and he cast it an accusing glance before getting up to answer.

133

*If I reach it before its fourth ring then the caller will have news of Laura.*

He did but they didn't.

'Leo?' He didn't recognise the female voice. 'It's Henryka.'

'Oh hi, Henryka. Everything OK?' He wondered why the Polish cleaning girl he'd occasionally shared coffee with at the end of his shift and the start of hers was phoning him and how she got his number.

'Mrs Baptiste told me to telephone you. Are you ill?'

'I'm fine, ' Leo answered in confusion. Then he pulled the closed blinds aside and noted the early morning sunlight. It was not 6.05 p.m. but 6.05 a.m and his shift was nearly over. Recovering quickly he added, 'Well, a bit under the weather. Migraine,' he added lamely.

'We were worried about you when you didn't come in. Don't worry, we will tell your relief that you went home early.'

'Thanks, Henryka. I'll see you tomorrow.' Leo put down the phone and sat back in front of the laptop, the conversation already forgotten. His stomach purred and he told himself he would work through one more file before he made himself some dinner.

* * *

Lunch with Ashley was always a three-hour affair but Leo had been strangely relieved to get a telephone call from her. Having raked the contents of Mutatkar's laptop he was down to the last couple of files and welcomed any interruption that would stall resigning himself to finding nothing. He accepted the invitation even though he hadn't slept for over twenty-four hours. The lack of temazepam made him feel like he could stay awake for hours but when she told him where she'd booked lunch Leo thought he'd fallen asleep at the laptop.

Chevalier's was buzzing when he got there and Ashley was waiting for him at a table in the front bar looking into a bowl of red wine. She stood up to kiss him as he tentatively removed his jacket.

'I know why you're doing this, Ash, but you've no idea how many times I've been back here already.'

'Not to eat though,' she said sitting down again. 'I've ordered for both of us.'

Leo sat and looked up the stairs behind Ashley to the area beyond. He wondered if she'd deliberately positioned them there.

'I couldn't get us a table upstairs at short notice.'

Leo saw Hektor emerge from behind the bar. He look harassed as usual and the lines on his Mediterranean features seemed a little deeper than the last time he'd seen him. Was there even an extra pound or two on his short frame? Nevertheless his silver grey hair was still immaculately squared around his tanned features and there was little to suggest that they'd celebrated his fiftieth birthday in Leo's other life.

Hektor leaned on the front of the bar and rested his hand on the thin waist of one of the bar staff while he talked to her. Everything seemed to be as it had been all those months ago and, for a split second, it was like inhabiting his old life again. He didn't want to make eye contact with Hektor though and returned his attention to Ashley.

'Lunch and banality, that's all I want.' She smiled and snapped a breadstick, handing him half.

He took it but placed it on his side plate and suddenly felt nauseous. It was the smell of the place. One aroma led to another and soon he would smell the sweaty interior of the interview room and the stale nicotine gum the investigating officer used to pulp in one side of his face. 'Thanks for trying to do this but this really doesn't feel right.' How could Ashley not understand that this was Laura's place, Laura's very last location? He rose but Ashley put her fingers round his wrist.

'Don't think this is easy for me either. Sit down,' she whispered firmly but even before he'd settled again he'd decided against telling her about Mutatkar. 'It's a room full of chairs and tables. People pass through it...good and bad.'

Leo didn't hear her but visualised Bookwalter stood at the top of the stairs in a delivery uniform. His shoulders tightened, almost in readiness for an impact of some kind.

'Let's try some meaningless chatter. How's work?'

He returned his gaze to her and registered how perfectly her fuchsia lip-gloss had been applied. She had on a tawny silk shirt and matching beads and her dark curls were once more in decorous disarray about her elegant face.

Being here with her wasn't right. After Hektor had been forced to suspend the immigrants in his staff and had taken it out on Leo, it had been an excuse to stop haunting the place. He should never have come back.

Ashley had clearly been waiting for an answer to her first question and raised her eyebrows as she tried another tack. 'Have you had any sort of contact with human beings apart from me?'

'Only Matty stalking me.'

'We all know about that. Stalking, I mean,' she added a little too hastily.

Leo thought he almost saw her bite her tongue. To Leo's knowledge, Ashley had very little to do with Matty except when they'd met at the wedding.

'Stalking or Matty's stalking?'

Ashley looked sheepish. 'OK, Matty's stalking.'

'So, are you going to make me beg for what you aren't telling me?'

Ashley used the action of refilling her water glass to break eye contact. 'Only what Laura told me.'

'Which was?'

'That Matty was capable of it.'

'But my brother was AWOL for most of the time Laura knew him. It's only since he moved in with Carla that he's been stalking me to play grown-ups with him.'

Ashley looked at him again and just nodded in hollow agreement as if she were considering whether she should tell him something.

'Ash...' he said, mock-threateningly.

'Pointless dragging things up now, particularly if you're on speaking terms with Matty.' She took her cue from his raised eyebrows. 'OK, there was a reason Matty was late to your wedding.' She pushed down and twisted the salt cellar so the tablecloth started to knot around it. 'He called at your house while you were waiting at the registry office.' She narrowed her eyes at the cellar.

'What for?' He felt his shoulders tighten.

'To...appeal...to Laura.'

'To not marry me?' said Leo jokingly.

'Yes.'

Leo sat back in his chair and his mind went utterly blank.

'And to marry him.' Ashley lifted her wine glass to her lips as if quickly concealing the source of the revelation.

Leo felt as if he was being suddenly pulled out of his mould. Ashley's pained face seemed to mirror what he felt on his own features and it was clearly something she'd dreaded telling him for a very long time.

'Ancient history,' she said and unsuccessfully tried to sound matter-of-fact.

'But news to me.' Something started to pool inside him but he wasn't sure if it was undiluted anger or pain.

'Laura didn't want to tell you because she knew how fragile things were between you and your brother.'

Leo didn't hear her. He was already spooling back the few occasions Matty had been in Laura's company. 'But Matty hardly knew her.'

'That's what was so bizarre. I didn't hear the conversation. Not that there was much of one anyway. Matty turned up at the front door and said he wanted to talk to Laura about a sensitive matter. Laura saw him in her room; she already had her dress on by then. Next thing I know, Matty is coming back down the stairs. I couldn't believe it when Laura told me what it had been about. Apparently, once she'd said no he'd turned on his heel and gone to join you at the registrar's.'

'Quatro staggioni.' The waitress announced what had just been placed in front of them but didn't hover with the black pepper grinder when she picked up the atmosphere from the table.

Ashley pulled a ring off her napkin. 'I'd only met Matty once or twice but watching him making his speech and acting throughout the day like it had never happened was just…unnerving.'

Leo thought that the day had been perfect. Laura

had said it had been and he suddenly felt idiotic for being so oblivious.

'Look, none of this effects how Laura felt about you,' Ashley said as if she were reading his mind. 'And Matty's happily settled now. He obviously had some... issues at the time.'

Leo felt aggression solidifying. So Matty had attempted to sabotage things like he always did. How he'd expected to do it that way was beyond him though. Perhaps it had made sense in his head, like all those well-timed vanishing acts he'd used to perform. Was he really so disturbed that he'd expected to steal Laura from him?

Now he felt foolish sitting in front of Ashley, knowing she'd been more aware of Matty's delusion than he'd ever been. And what he'd thought had been a happy day had been much less so for Laura. 'Thanks for lunch, Ash.'

'Leo, don't you dare go.'

But Leo was already bumping the back of his chair into the diner behind him

'I'll call you tonight, I promise. I can't...'

Leo held his breath until he'd made it to the door. Hektor was standing there chalking a special on the board as Leo scrabbled to find his coat from under the pile on the rack at the door. Hektor turned and began helping Leo put on his coat. Had he recognised him? His mind seemed to be elsewhere and Leo quickly turned his back on him so he could put his arms in the coat.

'Come back soon, sir.'

Leo didn't say a word and only breathed out when he was back outside in the fine spray of rain.

# CHAPTER 16

'Leo, it's Matty. We're worried about you and want to make sure you're OK. I don't know how to reach you bar kicking down your door. I've tried pretending that everything's normal but that obviously isn't working. Call me as soon as you hear this.'

The message prompted Leo to draw the curtains in the hallway window. The last thing he wanted was a surprise visit from his brother. Yeah, there certainly had been some pretence to normality. He'd never been convinced by Matty's sudden immersion in domestic bliss and now he wondered just how unbalanced he'd been when he called on Laura the day of their wedding.

He walked into the living room and stood in the middle of it, not knowing why he'd come in. The air was cold and he was suddenly aware of the rain mist that had soaked into his scalp trickling into his collar. His relationship with Laura, the only part of his existence that had been worthwhile, was long gone and now even that seemed to be warping into something ugly. He understood why Laura had kept Matty's proposal secret, but the absolute openness he'd always assumed they'd shared was suddenly in doubt. He looked around at the photos of Laura on the wall and wondered if she'd concealed anything else from him.

When Leo sat on his bed and opened his laptop he found an email from Bookwalter:

*Howdy doody*

*I fancy a new vacation*

*tall, freckle faced, chicken pox scar on left eyebrow*

*forward this email to ten friends*

*each of those friends must forward it to ten friends*

*maybe one of those friends of friends of friends will be one of my friends*

*if this email ends up in my inbox within a week I wont slit the bitchs throat*

*can you afford not to send this on to ten friends?*

*vk*

*Leo, if you cant make your mind up about taking that vacation Im going to have one of my own. Thought I'd run this email past you before I send it out there.*

Despite the provenance of the email it still,

oddly, unsettled Leo and he found himself willing Bookwalter's page to load up faster so he could log in to the private lounge. Bookwalter was online but Leo resisted the urge to type immediately and sat back, contemplating what to say before eventually opening their dialogue.

*So, how's the desalination protest?*

Leo remembered Bookwalter was spearheading the local opposition to the proposed plant and decided to ignore the email. If Bookwalter wanted to play mind fuck so could he.

There was a longer pause than normal before Bookwalter's reply constructed itself.

*Many apologies. I shouldnt be wasting your time with my local obsessions. Did you get my email?*

Again Leo circumvented the fact that he'd read it.

*Have visited the site address you forwarded and signed the petition.*

He hadn't.

An even longer pause than normal.

*Many thanks. It was very kind but I dont think people power has a snowballs chance of halting it.*

*How is Laura?*

Bookwalter's words were instant this time.

*Anxious. Have you spoken to Doctor Mutatkar about your travel arrangements?*

Leo leant back on his pillows and waited for him to press him further about the email but Bookwalter obviously knew he was deliberately evading.

Leo tapped in his response.

*Was hoping to ask him but he didn't make it.*

*Stuck in traffic?*

Again Bookwalter's reply was instant – as if he'd been waiting for an opportunity to use it.

Leo tried to be rational. Bookwalter could very easily have done an internet search for Mutatkar after he'd mentioned him and found the news item about his suicide and, of the comments he'd made in their earlier exchanges, all of them were vague enough to allow Leo to read whatever he wanted in to them.

*Dead.*

Leo had no desire to indulge Bookwalter's attempts at humour.

*Im so sorry. Was it sudden?*

*For his wife and daughter particularly.*

*I AM sorry.*

*Why? You didn't murder him and roll his car into traffic.*

*You know he was murdered?*

*Yes.*

Leo wondered if Bookwalter was genuinely surprised.

He waited for his answer and heard himself breathe out four times before it started to appear.

*Like all murder, it must have been committed to serve a purpose. If only to prove that nobody is as secure as they believe they are.*

Leo registered that Bookwalter was trying to cross reference Mutatkar's death to one of the pseudo-enigmatic observations he'd made when he'd had the dialogue with him from the doctor's bedsit. It was also an obvious allusion to his recent email. Leo waited for Bookwalter to elaborate.

*Everyone has a shelf life.*

For a moment, he almost had second thoughts about what he was about to type. He'd already made up his mind but he wondered if Bookwalter's email had sealed it.

*Looks like I'll be travelling alone then. I'm ready to see Laura now. How soon can you send me an air ticket?*

\* \* \*

'Mr Allan-Carlin, please.' Cleaves ran his hand over the prickles of his hair and lingered over the sparse patch on his scalp. His palm felt cool against it and he didn't care for the sensation.

'I'm afraid he's in a meeting.'

'He'll speak to me. Tell him it's Cleaves.'

He waited while the secretary put him on hold

and tried to identify the piece of classical muzak. His workdays were a far cry from his tours in the Special Forces and he often wondered if being left in a shallow grave in Mali for his gun-running activities would have been a better fate.

'This must be one of those rare emergencies when you contact me during business hours.' Joe Allan-Carlin sounded appropriately surly.

'Just one of those occasions, particularly as I've been trying to get hold of you since yesterday.'

'Make it quick.'

'Sharpe was back at Chevalier's yesterday.'

There was a brief pause. 'Doing what specifically?'

'Having lunch with his sister-in-law. Now he's left the country.'

'What?'

'Caught a flight to New Orleans. Maybe he's going on holiday. What do you want me to do?' Cleaves pushed through the revolving door of the airport and strode quickly back to his car that he'd left at the drop-off point.

Eventually, 'I don't suppose there's much we can do until he comes back.'

'Could be weeks. I'll see what I can find out in the meantime.' Cleaves thought about his expenses. Allan-Carlin was his full-time meal ticket. 'Maybe I should look in on things while he's away. Make sure his plants are watered.'

'Do whatever's necessary but don't call me until you've got something concrete.'

* * *

*Behind the frosted pane, the dark shape of the intruder moved unnaturally, his arm and shoulder frantically vibrating as the handle of the back door rattled. Leo struggled to keep his eyelids open but they locked shut as wood splintered and the handle clanged to the floor. He willed his hands to move so he could prise his eyes open but, as the door creaked, could feel no sensation in them.*

*He heard himself grunt with the exertion of trying to yank his eyes open with the muscles of his face and, for a brief moment, he could see the figure – a glimpse through the shutter of his vision as it briefly opened before snapping to darkness again. An impression of the figure was left on the black backdrop – a figure wearing a uniform. His lids were glued now but he could feel the presence of the intruder, breath and proximity. Footsteps halted at Leo.*

'Do you mind stowing your hand luggage under the seat in front of you?'

Leo found his eyes were open again and absorbing the face above him. The male air steward's expression was one of impatience. Leo shoved the bag under the seat in front with his foot and kicked it again for good measure.

'Thank you, sir.' The air steward continued his

149

checks past Leo's row. He pulled his bag out from under the seat again with the sides of his heels and allowed his feet to stretch out in the vacated gap. It was the third time he'd done it and was sure it wouldn't be long before the steward interrupted his sleep again.

After all of Bookwalter's entreaties he'd at least expected business class. But although his forthcoming host had seemed taken aback by Leo's request for the next available flight he had been highly efficient. Leo had been emailed his flight details less than half an hour later with promises that everything would be made ready for his arrival.

Leo didn't question what he was doing by allowing himself to be enticed by a man who had attempted to get himself imprisoned for a string of brutal murders he hadn't committed. He'd long since acknowledged Bookwalter as a delusional egocentric and had always managed to hold him at arm's length, like a snake handler with a glove and a pronged staff. But now he was exposing himself to something more dangerous than a mutual indulgence he was entirely unclear as to what either of their motives were.

The trip represented movement though – something his life had been devoid of – but was it in a direction he could easily find his way back from? He couldn't deny that he had an odd rapport with Bookwalter, one born from a shared obsession and self-imposed isolation but he really knew nothing of the man he was about to meet. Leo didn't know where Laura was, but he knew she wasn't where he was headed; but how could he not challenge Bookwalter on the claim he'd been making for so many months? How would Bookwalter possibly explain Laura's non-presence when he got there? He had to be careful and told himself that from the moment he touched down he had to be in complete control of every element of contact. As soon as he found himself in a situation that was otherwise, he would be buying his own ticket home.

Bookwalter had not only offered to pick Leo up at the airport but to put him up at his home for the duration of his stay. Leo had declined saying that he would book into a hotel first and then telephone Bookwalter so they could arrange a mutually satisfactory meeting place. Bookwalter had made several recommendations for places to stay and again offered to foot the bill but Leo told him he would make his own arrangements.

Two hours to touchdown. The lights were out and most people were snoozing under their blankets. Leo was too uneasy and skittish to sleep. According to Bookwalter he would be able to see Laura in less than twenty-four hours.

# CHAPTER 17

The sensation didn't seize him until he'd cleared customs and had walked through the main concourse of the airport. As soon as he hit the carpeted foyer though it was like a siren had gone off in the back of his head: Bookwalter was watching him. Every passenger had to walk across the area Leo was now dragging his case across and it was populated enough to afford sufficient cover for his arrival to be safely observed.

He resisted the temptation to look round but still half expected to make out Bookwalter in the host of faces that flashed by him. He felt the beginnings of panic and avoided eye contact. Bookwalter had booked the flight; he could so easily have taken it upon himself to head up a welcoming committee. The ridiculous notion of finding Laura standing with him lurched in his mind and left an acid sickness in his stomach. It couldn't happen here, not with him tired and vulnerable from the flight; he needed time to psyche himself up beforehand.

He thought about calling the number that Bookwalter had given him. He could tell him that he'd landed and nothing more. At least that way he would know if he was at the airport or not. He fumbled the paper with the details on from inside his leather jacket pocket and looked at the jumble of numbers. It was probably a cell number anyway.

He had to focus on getting out of here as quickly as possible. He strode faster and sensed somebody looking at him from the corner of his eye. He couldn't resist the reflex to turn. It was a short, Hispanic driver holding a card with somebody's surname on. A row of similar people stretched out to Leo's left and he dreaded seeing his own name materialise. He headed towards a desk to his right with a cab sign above it. It was occupied by a nicotine-stained woman, her hair permed into tiny coils.

'Welcome to N'awlins, sir. Where would you like to go today?'

Leo's mind was unresponsive so he fidgeted out another piece of paper from inside his jacket, all the while anticipating a hand on his shoulder. 'Hotel L'agneau.'

'Great place to stay,' she said cheerfully and almost convincingly. 'Join the line at C.'

It was sunny outside but a lot colder than he'd anticipated and as he dragged his case through the sliding doors a vaguely unpleasant smell pervaded the air, like something sour was evaporating. C was the only letter he could find. The line moved quickly though and he breathed a sigh of relief as soon as his case was loaded and he was sealed in the back of the cab. The cab driver lobbed some platitudes at him but Leo didn't hear them because his attention was fixed behind them until he was reassured that they hadn't been followed from the pick-up point.

Hotel L'agneau was in Barrack's Street on the north edge of the French Quarter and the journey there confirmed that the Mardis Gras celebrations of the previous few weeks were well and truly over. The streets were still littered with the debris though; plastic beer cups, beads and streamers were still being swept out of the gutters. Leo identified the aroma as stale booze and urine. Hurricane Katrina or not, New Orleans was still taking care of business and Leo had landed slap bang in the middle of the hangover.

The hotel had the traditional New Orleans frontage but the recently applied paint couldn't disguise the malignant rust on its wrought-iron railings. Its white, seventeenth-century frontage looked infected with it as well and as the cab pulled up, Leo waited for the liver-spotted exterior to cough and splutter. It would suffice though because it was at the opposite pole to

155

Bookwalter's neighbourhood. He was in Crescent City, which was actually just outside New Orleans, eastbound on Route 90 which crossed the stretch of the Mississippi that Leo was glad separated them.

His room was 'tucked nicely in back' as the old boy with worn shiny trousers informed him, as if it was a selling point. But Leo didn't register the sloping floors and the furniture leaning away from the walls; he just dumped his case on the bed where it remained unopened and looked down on the overgrown courtyard through his small window. It felt like late afternoon and when he looked at his watch that he'd set to New Orleans time as they'd landed, he was surprised to find he was right. Four thirty – his intuition for daylight hours seemed to be returning.

The ball was in his court. He was to decide where and when their meeting would take place.

\* \* \*

Laveau's Chicken Shack was a chicken and biscuits chain and at dinnertime it was full of families gorging on that day's meal deal. The din was incredible. Leo ordered something at random, took his tray and sat at a table in the middle of the restaurant. He'd wandered around a few bars but wanted the venue to be as populated as possible. The drinking holes in the French Quarter were all dimly lit and Laveau's Chicken Shack had no walls, only windows.

Late afternoon sun was still making the diners squint and as he glanced at the contents of his tray he tried to remember the last time he'd eaten. It didn't feel like it would happen anytime soon either. He'd telephoned Bookwalter from a call box and told him where they were to meet. Bookwalter had sounded dubious but agreed and said he would be there in twenty minutes. Had that been for Leo's benefit or was he actually watching him?

*Do you feel impregnable?*

With an ocean between them it had been easy for Leo to believe that he was out of his correspondent's grasp but now he was here, separated only by minutes, Leo felt like Bookwalter already had the advantage. It was his domain. He looked around at the people distracted by their food. He felt susceptible in the presence of more than one person at home let alone sat amongst a society that felt entirely alien to him. Leo felt quite unnerved by how single-minded the process of eating seemed and there seemed to be no chance that his gaze would be returned by anyone else.

He focused on the grey chicken and the bag of deep fried whatever-the-hell-it-was on his tray while he sucked something ice cold and sugary through a straw. He felt it cold in the middle of his forehead and fixed his attention on the entrance. He'd spent some time in the queue and wondered how many minutes had elapsed since he'd got off the phone to Bookwalter.

*If Bookwalter walks in now, Laura is here.*

Outside, the flow of pedestrians seemed to increase as the sun burning the urine off the sidewalks began to lose its intensity. Another family walked in: middle-aged father in a bright shirt, shorts and flip-flops, the mother wearing hardly anything when she really should have – her tanned cellulite folded over the top of her denim hot pants as another roll of flab tried to meet it from beneath her knotted midriff T-shirt. Their bored, nearly teenage kids looked as happy to be in the place as they did. They stopped a few feet from the counter and squinted at the menu and then Mom walked forward dragging the kids to make their choices. Dad stayed where he was and then Leo realised that he wasn't with the woman and children. He had simply walked in behind them. It was Bookwalter.

At that moment Bookwalter spotted Leo, rolled his eyes and slopped up to the table. 'Surely you're not eating here?' Like watching his onscreen dialogue, his drawl seemed to frustrate the speed at which he wanted to speak and Leo could see the intelligence in his blue-grey eyes flickering like a hard drive.

Bookwalter put his hands on his hips and looked away to study the menu over the counter again, breathing heavily. Leo felt uneasy as he took his time to survey it.

Here was a man who clearly enjoyed his food. From the pictures and footage online, Leo had seen little of the area below his shoulders, and was quite surprised at how rotund the man was. Leo estimated his height to be no more than five foot six. His features were undoubtedly fuller as well. The hair that Leo had suspected had been in short supply on his head – because of the beret he wore in the photos – was actually quite abundant. He was definitely thinning but a stubborn and significant jetty of auburn hair extended in a V shape from the back of his head where his longer fronds covered his ears and just touched the collar of his orange Hawaiian shirt. The new addition to his face was a moustache of the same colour that drooped over his top lip, the ends touching the edge of his chin.

'Do you like seafood?' Bookwalter asked eventually as if it were highly unlikely that he did.

'Uh, yeah—' Leo didn't know whether to stand and offer his hand but it seemed the time for a physical greeting was over.

Relief flooded Bookwalter's face and he wiped at it with a handkerchief that he had balled in his hand. 'Let's go to King Crawdaddy's then. You have to taste their shrimp etouffee. I'm buying.' His eyes narrowed earnestly at Leo.

The offer seemed so casual and Leo almost welcomed the opportunity to be out of the noise. 'Here's fine... if you don't mind.' Why had he been thinking about shaking the guy's hand? He should have been over the

159

table with his hands around his throat for posting the picture of Laura on the internet. But their surroundings seemed to preclude anything other than the glib and Leo already felt his apprehension sapping.

Bookwalter's eyes shifted sideways; he frowned and then shrugged theatrically. 'Sure, whatever you say.' His words trickled slowly as oil but Leo wondered if he'd been favoured with a caricature of simple 'Awlins to put him at his ease. He sat down opposite him and Leo wondered if the fact that his frame was barely supported by the plastic chair was the real motive for him wanting to leave. As he waggled his buttocks, it was difficult to believe that this was a man capable of anything more than passing the time of the day, let alone the allusive retorts he'd been feeding to Leo.

It was bizarre but it felt like Leo already knew him. Having seen only jpegs and grainy images, and heard his voice filtered through a speaker and the tenth rate quality of his YouTube clips, it still felt like they met up like this on a regular basis. He seemed somehow smaller in stature than Leo expected, despite the pounds that hung off his frame, but otherwise his presence was unnervingly familiar – as if they'd spent months sat in the same proximity but never looking up from their computers. Even the smell of Bookwalter's aftershave smelt commonplace.

Perhaps putting people at ease was his trick and it was only by making a concerted effort to remember what had been trickling down the internet from Bookwalter to Leo that he resisted the sudden temptation to feel utterly unthreatened.

For a moment the idea flashed through his mind that this was a huge mistake. He hadn't doubted that from the moment he'd agreed to come but Leo was suddenly seized by the notion that everything was a massive misunderstanding. A frown would converge on Bookwalter's ingenuous features as soon as he started talking about Laura and, somehow, Leo felt it must transpire they had both been duped by some third party who'd had them talking at cross purposes for all this time.

'Good flight?' Bookwalter chewed on something invisible.

Leo nodded quickly.

'Where are you staying?'

'In town.' Leo tried not to feel uncomfortable about being so terse to the man who had paid for his trip.

'You should go see the Superdome while you're here. Since the floods it's become our most spiritual landmark.' Again, Bookwalter eyes were fixed on him earnestly and left only the sound of his straining nostrils between them.

'How's the desalination protest?'

'Futile.' Bookwalter looked irked by the question, folded his arms on the table and looked sideways. It looked as if he were about to share something intimate but when he turned it appeared he was waiting for Leo to ask him a more palatable question. Leo tried to think of one but the very fact that he was swapping chitchat with a man who claimed to be holding Laura captive had fused his tongue to the top of his mouth. Bookwalter sniffed and dabbed his face with his handkerchief again. It wasn't even hot in the restaurant but he looked as if he'd got sunburnt since he'd sat down. Probably high blood pressure. 'She's so excited you came.'

Leo should have been nodding sceptically but felt only an internal hiss of relief. Whatever Bookwalter did to try and mitigate his claim in the future, Leo, momentarily, didn't care. He had justified his presence in this place, in Bookwalter's company and, for however brief it was, he had a purpose. It would be over as quickly as everything else he'd done to find Laura, and he knew that this was maybe a shorter dead end than Mutatkar. For now, though, it meant that they were going to talk about Laura and that was something nobody else wanted to do anymore.

'When can I see her?'

'Whenever you want,' Bookwalter said matter-of-factly. He leant back in his chair and lifted his arms as if expecting to be able to drape them along something behind him, then let them drop back into his lap, slouching forward again. He looked utterly uncomfortable, like a petulant child who hadn't been allowed to get down from the table. 'Have you finished here?' He nodded towards Leo's full tray.

'I'm not going to be eating, if that's what you mean.'

'Let's go then.'

'Go?' DON'T GO. DON'T GO.

'Well...you said you want to go see her.'

Leo certainly hadn't been prepared for this. 'Where?' It wasn't the answer his brain wanted to give.

'I'll take you there.' Bookwalter examined the panic on Leo's face with amusement. 'Look, we'll call two cabs. You follow mine. I take you anywhere you feel uncomfortable and you can ask your driver to turn around.' Bookwalter produced his telephone.

'Why didn't she come with you?'

Bookwalter's smile broadened and Leo didn't like it. It was just a spasm, a movement of muscles that allowed him to see his stained teeth. 'She's waiting.'

Leo shook his head for effect. LEAVE NOW. 'And what would you do in my position?'

'I probably wouldn't come.' Bookwalter got to his feet. 'It's your decision though. I don't want to pressure you into doing anything you don't want to but I'm trying to make this as easy as possible. All I can tell you is you're in no danger whatsoever. Someone know you're here?'

'Of course.' THEY DON'T.

'I'm not going to drive you anywhere remote. There's plenty of people about and we'll be in two separate cars.' Bookwalter pulled his foot out of one of his flip-flops and picked at a piece of dirt embedded in his sole. While he stood on one foot, he waggled precariously on the spot and a fold of skin appeared under his chin to block his breathing. 'It's what you came for, Leo.' It was the first time he'd heard Bookwalter utter his name but he wasn't meeting his eye now. 'You can come now or I can give you some time to think about it.'

Bookwalter was right. Whatever deception had been prepared, Leo wasn't going to be able to dismiss it as such until he'd seen it with his own eyes. He'd envisaged all sorts of intricate scenarios; selecting a meeting place that he could monitor from a safe distance to make sure that Bookwalter didn't have any accomplices, moving him from one venue to the next via telephone calls and meeting him on moving public transport – but it was all a product of having watched too many movies. Bookwalter wanted to show him something and Leo had to go. 'OK.' DON'T GO. DON'T GO.

Bookwalter used the action of dialling his cell to keep his eyes from Leo's but a suggestion of a smirk folded his moustachioed top lip over his lower one.

'I'll call the cabs.' Leo pulled out his own cell.

Bookwalter looked up and raised one eyebrow. 'O...K.' But his expression said it didn't make any difference.

'I'll call them now and meet you outside. I have another call to make to another party after that. I'll be having a running commentary with them throughout and reporting where we go.'

Bookwalter raised his hands in compliance. 'However you want to run things...I'll be outside.'

# CHAPTER 18

When the cabs arrived Bookwalter walked back into the restaurant and gave Leo another stained smile and the thumbs up. It felt like they were going away on a fishing trip together. Luckily for Leo he was in the middle of leaving a message for Ashley so Bookwalter registered this fact before slopping back out of the restaurant.

'Ashley...pick up if you're there. Ashley? I know this is weird but I'm in...I'm on holiday. Just need some time on my own at the moment. I'll call you as soon as I get back.'

Leo terminated the call but kept his handset open. How could he tell Ashley he'd come to meet Bookwalter? He knew exactly what she'd say and she'd have been right. The last thing he needed was the voice of reason to persuade him to take his cab straight back to the airport. He kept the phone pressed to his ear and walked to the exit.

Outside Bookwalter was sat in the back of a car wiping his face and Leo walked up to his window and gestured for him to open it. The glass dropped and Bookwalter raised his eyebrows.

'Where are we headed?'

'Just follow me to Crescent City. Your cab driver will tell you exactly where you're going.'

Leo got into the back of the cab behind Bookwalter's. 'Could you follow the car in front?' His black driver looked at him in the rear-view mirror and nodded almost indiscernibly. He was bald and Leo couldn't tell how old he was. Bookwalter's car eased out of its parking space and Leo's did the same, entering the sluggish traffic and rolling only a few yards before it stopped behind the tailback of Chevys and Outlanders heading for home. Leo could see the back of Bookwalter's head but kept the phone to his ear. Nobody knew where he was going. Nobody knew he was even in the States.

They crawled along Route 90 and eventually crossed the Mississippi into Bookwalter's neck of the woods. Leo tried to take in the scenery while he listened to the dead phone rub against his ear.

The name Romain Street seemed familiar to Leo but both cars already started to slow down before he realised that he recognised it from the details Bookwalter had emailed him. This was their destination and he was surprised to find himself in front of a block of white-fronted, modern houses with a stretch of green separating them from the sidewalk, the individual gardens delineated only by low rows of ornamental bricks angled out of the grass. A handful of children were playing noisily out front and Leo waited as Bookwalter got out of the car and paid his cab driver. The car pulled away and Bookwalter gestured with both hands for Leo to follow him up the drive to the end house.

Leo opened his door still with the phone to his ear and put his finger in his other as if the noise of the kids was drowning out the conversation he was having. He nodded and mumbled into the phone while Bookwalter beckoned him again as if he were directing a reversing lorry. Leo's cab driver rolled down his side window and frowned at the phone conversation that had only begun since his passenger had got out of the car.

'Do you mind waiting? I'll be three minutes. If I'm not back in that time I'll pay you an extra hundred dollars to come in and get me.'

The cab driver's frown deepened and Leo turned to where Bookwalter had stopped halfway up the drive, turning his hands upwards in a gesture of 'what's the delay?' He turned back to the cab driver and looked into his eyes. He was younger than he thought. 'It's nothing illegal. I just need you as a witness. Two hundred dollars?'

The cab driver nodded and reluctantly turned off his engine. Leo walked to where Bookwalter was, cutting the corner of the lawn and stepping over the barrier of bricks. He snapped the phone shut and Bookwalter showed him his teeth again.

'Come on, Leo. There's somebody who can't wait to see you.'

Bookwalter's house smelt of baking. It hit Leo as soon as he walked in through the glass front door and he again wondered if it was another of his host's devices for putting him at his ease.

'Mind if I leave this front door open?'

Bookwalter kicked off his flip-flops and turned, a look of bemusement on his face. 'Whatever makes you comfortable, Leo.'

He'd had the same smirk on his face when Leo had reluctantly agreed to accompany him. Leo was beginning to think it was because Bookwalter recognised the fear in him – and that, he had long surmised, was what his host thrived on. The expression also seemed to suggest that Leo was in no danger and that it was comically entertaining for Bookwalter to witness Leo being so hyper cautious. DON'T EVEN BEGIN TO THINK THAT.

He took in the interior of Bookwalter's home. Not only was its populated location unexpected – the sounds of children playing and suburban bustle following them

170

through the door – but it seemed genuinely warm and welcoming. Leo had envisaged him living in a trailer or a single apartment, but the hallway that stretched in front of him had terracotta walls and immaculate yellow Aztec design carpets indicating an owner who was fiercely house proud.

Bookwalter padded down the hallway and walked into the first door on his left. Leo looked back out of the front door and could still see the cab driver glancing at his watch.

*If I'm not back to the car in three minutes it means Laura is here.*

He dismissed the thought and followed; he could make out the sound of an oven door opening.

Leo found himself in an equally spotless, spacious and modern kitchen, all washed out blue cupboards and chrome and the baking smell twice as inviting. A slim woman was standing at the central breakfast bar with her back to him: long dark hair, black T-shirt, denim shorts and bare feet. Her hands were slipped inside two huge oven gloves which she was using to rest a baking tray on the black marble-effect counter.

It couldn't be Laura. She was the right build, the right height but her legs were too tanned, her hair too different.

'Pumpkin, say hello.'

The woman turned with a slitted smile at the ready. She was barely a woman, probably only in her late teens. Her features were Hispanic, her nose hooky but her young face still quite beautiful. Large hooped earrings looked as if they counter-balanced her head. 'Hi,' she said shyly and it appeared to be more than she was used to saying. She turned back to the counter.

'She's a little busy. Her name's Perfecta. I don't know how I'd survive without her.' Bookwalter snaked a finger into the crook of her neck and her shoulder lifted and crushed it there.

She giggled. Unlikely as it was, she appeared to be Bookwalter's girlfriend. Or perhaps he had a very intimate arrangement with his housekeeper. What was she, eighteen...nineteen?

'Looks like she's baked some bizcochitos in your honour. We didn't eat out so we might be needing some of your pot roast.' Bookwalter leant against her back so he could take one from the tray, his hefty body weight crushing her against the counter. Bookwalter turned, tossing the biscuit into his mouth before gesturing for Leo to follow him out. 'You'll stay for dinner, right? Come on, there's somebody else you should meet.'

Bookwalter led Leo through the hallway and up a flight of stairs carpeted in the same yellow. Bookwalter puffed and panted in front of him and Leo briefly glanced back down the hallway to the waiting cab at the end of the drive before he followed.

His host waited for him at the top of the stairs and then stepped to one side as he reached the last stair.

Leo found himself on a similarly carpeted landing and Bookwalter cautiously used his knuckles to knock one of the bedroom doors open.

'Permission to enter,' said a voice from within. Bookwalter cringed and squinted his eyes as if expecting his presence to be unwelcome and then relaxed his features as he pushed it wider. 'Got a visitor for you.'

Bookwalter's frame blocked Leo's view through the doorway. From the angle of his head, Leo could see that whoever was being addressed seemed to be somewhere immediately inside the room. Bookwalter shuffled and shimmied his body forward and around the edge of the door to allow Leo to enter behind him. Inside the small room sat a man in front of a computer.

Man? Perhaps not quite. He had the same moustache as Bookwalter that curled down to the edge of his chin, but his was black. However, even though his facial hair suggested otherwise, he looked no older than sixteen. Dark hairs sprouted from his neck and threw a shadow over the bottom half of his face and only a small area around his eyes seemed without follicles. The hair on his head had been raked and braided into a black ponytail but that failed to rein in all the stray wiry hairs around it. Other than that he was the spitting image of Bookwalter although his paunch was even broader than his father's. A large bag of tortilla chips lay beside his keyboard and beside that a bottle of

Sprite that had been sucked inward. The room smelt of bubblegum and BO. 'This is Toby, in-house designer of my website.'

'Hey.' Toby leant forward slightly and Leo grasped the moist fingers that had been extended to him. He maintained eye contact with Leo.

'He's never away from his post and monitors the traffic 24/7. He's just updating the profiles pages which is why your visit is such good timing.' Bookwalter drawled.

'We're giving the Laura page a major makeover. Soon she's going to be more popular than the other UK victims.' Toby's voice sounded like it hadn't quite broken and his higher pitched twang sounded like a speeded-up version of his father's. Leo was aghast; he wasn't sure which was more tragic: what Bookwalter did to earn money or the fact that he'd involved his son. It was time to leave, time to re-enter reality.

He suddenly wanted to be home, wanted to see Ashley and let her dissect his misguided visit. Leo looked around the room at the posters on the wall. At first he'd assumed they were the usual collage of rock idols and movie images but every one of them had an ecological conscience – images of petrified forests and dead seabirds with slogans of outrage underlining them.

Twenty-four/seven? Then *this* was the boy he'd been talking to – this teenager. No wonder Bookwalter had no time for the desalination protest – it was his son who had brought it into their dialogues. Suddenly Leo felt marooned from Laura and any last vestiges of leading a life that dignified her memory.

# Chapter 19

What was Laura doing right now? It was a question he asked himself umpteen times a day. What was Laura doing at this precise moment? Sleeping, eating, crying, breathing? Was she imprisoned, was she in pain? Leo usually managed to stopper what lay beyond those possibilities – was she dead, was she buried, wrapped in bin liners, decomposed – but his desperate journey here had now removed it.

This signified the end of the slimmest of chances of ever finding Laura alive. It was why he'd resisted taking Bookwalter up on his offer for so long. However unlikely it seemed, Bookwalter had always been a last option. Now that had been extinguished as quickly as he'd suspected, Leo had to face up to doing what Ashley wanted him to do – to let go of Laura.

Toby clicked his mouse and the Laura page Leo had visited so many times filled the monitor – her beautiful face stared out at them and Leo had never felt less worthy of her.

'We're overhauling the whole site,' Bookwalter continued. 'It's a continual battle with the search engines so we want to beef up the content and intensify the detail on the click-through pages. That's where you come in.' Leo could smell Bookwalter's acrid breath when he spoke. It was like stale parmesan.

Leo's only thought was of leaving but, momentarily, he couldn't remember how he'd got there.

'Show him what he needs to see, Toby.'

Toby closed the window they were looking at and opened another that had been minimised in the task bar. A disturbing image filled the screen: a darkened room with somebody spotlit and tied to a chair. The figure's shaved head was bowed but Leo could tell that the bound, emaciated body – dressed in an ill-fitting boiler suit – was female.

The room was silent except for Bookwalter's nasal breathing. 'And I'm expected to believe that's my wife?' Leo didn't take his eyes off the monitor.

Neither Bookwalter nor Toby spoke.

The figure moved her right shoulder slightly and Leo looked at the time display below it. He didn't need to look at his watch to know that it would coincide. Suddenly, from downstairs came the sound of voices.

His cab driver had been as good as his word and it sounded like Perfecta was doing her best to placate him.

'Looks like my time's up, guys. Anything else to say before I put this into the hands of the police? '

Bookwalter briefly closed his eyes as if trying to keep his patience in check. 'What do you see, Leo?'

'A woman who could be anybody tied to a chair.'

'Exactly. So what crime has been perpetrated here exactly?'

Leo still hadn't moved his eyes from the screen.

'What if I told you she's willingly tied to that chair and, even if you didn't believe that, do you think she'd really come to any harm when she's currently being watched by 722 people.'

Leo found the counter at the bottom of the page.

'Johnny!' Perfecta obviously had her hands full with the cab driver but Leo's attention darted back to the image.

'Toby, help out downstairs.'

Toby grunted reluctantly while he unstuck himself from his leather swivel chair and squeezed past Leo.

'There are a hell of a lot of worse things being done legally to people on the internet... Subscription services for members like ours are so that consenting adults can watch or participate. You've only got to do a quick search of the BDSM sites to get a flavour of what's permissible...even within our own shores.' Bookwalter reeled it off like a carefully rehearsed sales pitch. 'I bet a lot of those people don't care if it's Laura or not. What pops people's corn is their own business. Fact is, the law enforcement of this community is more than familiar with John Bookwalter and, however much it displeases me, it would take a hell of a lot more than this for them to ever perceive me as any kind of real threat.'

'You really expect me to believe that this is Laura?'

'Depends on how much you want her to be Laura. You must at least acknowledge it as a possibility, otherwise you wouldn't be here.'

'You think that's the reason I'm here?' Leo wondered if he really had another excuse. Whatever it was he'd fantasised about doing to Bookwalter when he met him in the flesh, however – his desire to punish him for living off Leo's misery and the pain of the other victims – seemed unthinkable in this environment. 'You know nothing of me or of my agenda. What exactly is yours?'

'If I had on my Vacation Killer head I'd say I want to trap you like I did her. But with this business head on I'd say all I want is a little of your time. In exchange for that I guarantee I'll prove to you whether she is or she isn't Laura beyond a shadow of a doubt.'

'I think we could prove that now.'

'Not with my consent.' Bookwalter clicked the window shut and Leo suddenly resisted the urge to laugh. He couldn't see how Bookwalter could possibly juggle the reality of family life with his world of selective and lucrative delusion. Standing face-to-face it was virtually impossible to summon the rage he felt towards him for using Laura and the other victims to populate his commercial fantasy. 'Sounds like there's somebody downstairs who's very insistent on seeing you, Leo.'

Leo left Bookwalter breathing over the computer and headed downstairs.

Toby and Perfecta were blocking the progress of the cab driver who was now halfway up the hallway.

'Your three minutes is up. Tell these people what I'm doing here.' Sweat was pouring from his face which was set determinedly.

'Thanks for waiting but I think we're OK...'

The cab driver's shoulders sagged backwards but Toby and Perfecta's hands remained against his chest. 'You won't be needing me to stay?'

'No. Thank you.'

'OK then...' The cab driver remained where he was and raised his eyebrows.

'Oh...' Leo fumbled his wallet out of his jeans and pulled the cab fare plus the two hundred he owed and passed it through Toby and Perfecta.

The cab driver snatched the notes, turned on his heel and left Leo alone with the family.

# CHAPTER 20

Leo was sitting in Bookwalter's oriental garden, sipping the glass of iced tea that Perfecta had made for him before she'd gone back indoors. Bookwalter was showering and Toby had returned to his workspace.

The garden of stepped lilies and peonies was sheltered from the wind by a high red brick wall and the only sound was the water churning around the bamboo water wheel in the pond at its centre. Leo observed the handful of koi leisurely gliding into each other, then looked across at the swimming pool and jacuzzi on a raised platform at the end of the lawn. Everything looked a little cramped – as if the wealth was rapidly outgrowing its dimensions.

Whatever Bookwalter wanted from Leo he doubted that it was anything beyond using him to legitimise his ludicrous claims to infamy. It looked to be a full-time living for Bookwalter – a family business that needed to keep on delivering. He seemed to be the ultimate example of an anti-celebrity – famous and dependent on the patronage of warped sickos and people with too much time on their hands who took great delight in according cult status to unfortunates and lunatics. Multiply those people the world over and it wasn't inconceivable that serious money could be made from offering to cut in the advertisers on his spurious popularity.

Underneath Leo's anaemic mortification, however, there was a resounding sense of relief. Bookwalter's pathetic attempts to perpetuate his claims were laughable and the apprehension that he'd been feeling ever since he got on the plane had rapidly dissolved. The duplicity was as much his as Bookwalter's – he'd disregarded his own intuition and allowed himself to be hoodwinked, and for that reason he summoned most of the disgust for himself.

Leo wondered if Perfecta and Toby held down jobs or if perpetuating the Vacation Killer actually kept the wolf from the door for the entire family unit. How much of their lifestyle was skimmed off the back of shattered lives and events they had no connection to? He was determined to halt Bookwalter's set up, pull the plug on his whole offensive little enterprise. Doing that would at least be the beginnings of a justification of his involvement with him – a positive course of action that would have an actual repercussion. Maybe that way he could begin to make amends for sullying his and Laura's lives by even being associated with him.

Bookwalter was undoubtedly right; there was probably nothing the authorities could do. Not even the live image Leo'd been shown could be classed as illegal. It could still all be explained away as an elaborate performance as could everything his host accused himself of. He looked around and speculated as to how the family had lived before the Vacation Killer had murdered his first victim. Was Bookwalter as brain damaged as he'd always suspected or had everything been coldly calculated from the moment he'd walked into the precinct and attempted to confess?

Perfecta returned with the tray of home-baked cookies and set them down on the patio table, tightening her lips into a smile before turning to leave again.

'You have a lovely home, Mrs Bookwalter.'

She reached the patio door again before she decided to turn and answer his unspoken question. 'We're not married.'

Leo thought about his next question but she answered it before he'd asked.

'I've lived under his roof for over three years now but he's never asked me.' Her eyeballs rolled briefly upwards and Leo wondered if it was weary affection or a genuine gripe out of earshot.

Idly, Leo wondered what had happened to Toby's mother. 'The three of you seem very happy.'

Perfecta nodded a little too quickly as if pleasantly surprised to be engaged in conversation. 'There are many things I would like but...' She cut herself off. 'We're very fortunate.' The words didn't sound like her own.

'And you're quite comfortable with John being...'

She smiled this time, the first genuine one he'd seen. 'It's not so different to live with a celebrity.' She seemed certain of this. Not that Bookwalter had ordinary habits but of the fact that he was most definitely famous. Her smile turned into a smirk. 'I tell people he is as messy as any other man.'

So Perfecta was star-struck. It certainly explained why she would happily clean up after Bookwalter and Toby.

She seemed to detect his bemusement and the smile left without a trace. 'He's always provided well for me.'

'Does it not bother you how he makes his living?'

'He's always provided well for me.' She shrugged her shoulders and this time her hostility showed she really meant it.

'So, you know everything he and Toby do?'

She pursed her lips before she answered. 'I'm his bookkeeper. There's nothing he does without consulting me. John admits he's hopeless with money so he leaves everything to me. I pay the bills, I put food in mouths but I know who keeps me alive.' She made as if to leave and then turned and looked him sourly in the eye. 'And what do you do?'

'It's a good question.'

She waited for Leo to finish answering but he already had. He looked into his iced tea and waited for a response but realised she was gone. He was about to take another sip when he was blinded by the flash of a camera.

Turning, he found that Bookwalter and Toby had replaced Perfecta at the open patio doors. Bookwalter beamed. He looked different and Leo realised it was not only because he'd now changed into a darker blue Hawaiian print shirt but because his hair was slicked back from his shower and he now wore spectacles which magnified his eyes comically. Toby stood beside him with the camera.

'Don't take pictures of me,' Leo said definitively. Was this part of Bookwalter's package deal? Did he want the pair of them shaking hands?

'Later, Toby.' Bookwalter said it as if it was a certainty and blinked twice at Leo through his thick lenses. 'Dinner's almost ready.' He clacked into the garden in his flip-flops and pulled back the wooden chair opposite Leo. 'Sorry we can't offer you anything stronger but we don't keep beer or liquor in the house. Perfecta doesn't want me tempted back to my old ways.' Leo noticed he had a black leather document wallet in his hand and he laid it on the table as if it were a fait accompli.

'Am I to sign something?'

'Yes.' Bookwalter adjusted the specs on the bridge of his nose and unzipped the wallet. 'Once you've read it of course. I have a copy for you to take away. Absorb it in your hotel room. That's, of course, if you haven't changed your mind about staying with us.'

After what he'd just been shown upstairs, the offer seemed even more ludicrous. 'I haven't. I just wanted to make sure you're covering my imminent flight back.'

'You know I'm good for those tickets. You can return any time you want but the fact is if you weren't intrigued by my proposition you wouldn't still be sitting in my home.' Bookwalter pulled out a fat document and flipped it open to the first page.

He was right. Could he really dismiss the image he'd been shown? Yes, just, almost – but surely Bookwalter's bargaining position didn't rest on the grainy image of somebody who so obviously could have been anybody. Or maybe Bookwalter knew that however insubstantial it was it would still be enough. 'What exactly do you think you have that I want?'

Bookwalter's eyes slipped sideways and then he looked openmouthed at Leo as if the question was academic. 'The truth.'

'And that's what you're supplying.'

'Whether you believe me or not, what I'm offering is a cross section of what I do here. It's not everybody

I invite in like I've done you.' Bookwalter seemed genuinely hurt.

'Look, maybe you've reached the stage where you can't even admit your own lies to yourself but can't you see what you and your family do is monstrous?'

'Have we not given you hope?'

Leo was momentarily dumbstruck. 'Is that what you're in this business for?'

'Partly. I think the site...helps people.'

'Help? Is that what you were doing when you claimed to hold my wife prisoner?'

Bookwalter licked his lips while he considered his response. 'We're a Christian family, Leo. Everyone's got to earn a living and we help who we can in the process. Don't tell me our conversations weren't a comfort to you.'

'So let me understand what you're saying. You're a Christian serial killer who claims responsibility for the mutilation and murder of innocent people to make a few dollars from the internet. And you can square all of that because you've been psychoanalysing me.'

'Not a few dollars, Leo.' Bookwalter's eyes sparkled now and he seemed entirely unscathed by what Leo had said. 'And if you'll just let me explain what I have in front of me you'll understand how this can work for everyone.'

'So when you show me that the person, whoever it is, tied to that chair isn't the person you've been claiming it to be, when you take away my only reason for ever being associated with you while you've been blackmailing the desperate and weak part of me, you really don't expect me to do everything in my power to put you where you seem desperate to go.'

'You could have put a stop to this months ago; why didn't you?' Bookwalter licked his thumb and turned another page of the document, raising his eyebrows to study the print. 'It wasn't me doing all the talking.'

'No. Toby did a lot of it.'

Bookwalter looked up and again he looked wounded. 'Toby only ever filled in when I was indisposed.'

'So who was it in Chevalier's – you or your teenage son?'

Bookwalter narrowed his eyes as if Leo's comment was noxious. 'Nobody could have written that but me.'

'Seeing as you've never left the state of Louisiana, how could I ever have doubted you?'

'There are many things you know about me but even more you don't.'

Now it was like they were at their keyboards again, Bookwalter rattling off his tenebrous lines of evasion.

'It doesn't sound as if you're even considering this. It could be the opportunity to answer all the questions you've been putting to me since you first made contact.'

'I first made contact with you because I wanted the photo of Laura removed.'

190

'The photo that you'd never seen before. Not curious about how I came by it?'

It sounded to Leo like Bookwalter was trying to use any scant piece of leverage he had. 'So, just what is in this document that you expect me to sign?' Leo wondered if it was too thick to tear from top to bottom in front of Bookwalter's blinking eyes.

'Take it away, look it over...'

'Précis it for me.'

'Very well. This document allows you access to every classified level of *stillonvacation.com*. Not only that but it grants you exclusive admittance to my personal archive and database, as well as a small percentage of gross from the site—'

'More importantly, I'm sure, what does it grant you?'

'Complete immunity from prosecution by you or your representatives.' Bookwalter fixed him with his magnified blue-grey eyes and bit down earnestly on his lip so his red moustache folded into his mouth.

# CHAPTER 21

Leo was momentarily speechless. 'And why would you need that?'

'One less suit for me to worry about.'

'So, what exactly are you planning for the future?'

'Like Toby said, we're overhauling the whole site.'

Leo visualised the incarcerated figure shifting in the chair. 'And you didn't think I'd have a problem with this.'

'The Vanderplows certainly didn't.'

The name didn't register with Leo for a few seconds, but he had to take a sharp intake of breath when he realised who Bookwalter was referring to. Jill Vanderplow was the Vacation Killer's second victim. She'd disappeared from Windham County, Connecticut on the 13th March 2006 and her jawbone had been mailed to the local police four days later.

'Like most of the victim's families, they actually still believe that it was Bonsignore that took their daughter, but life goes on and they still need to put food on the table. At least my site keeps Jill's memory alive.'

'They signed this?' Leo hated the incredulity in his own voice. Bookwalter had to be lying.

'They're the only ones who have so far. I've had flat turndowns from the other families. The Andersons are taking advice though.'

Estelle Anderson was the mother of two from New Hampshire who suffered the same fate. 'They've given you their blessing to claim responsibility for their murders?'

'I claim it regardless. I'm an inconsequential lunatic to them but why not extract something positive from one of the hundreds of sites that have become intrigued by events that were entirely beyond their control.'

Leo found himself on his feet. 'Fuck this.'

'You won't sign?' It sounded like Bookwalter had something rehearsed for this eventuality but Leo wasn't about to give him the opening.

'This is beyond vile opportunism. I can't believe I actually allowed you to lure me here.'

Bookwalter didn't rise though. He sat with his hand on the document wallet and focused on Leo's midriff. 'Don't dismiss me.' He said it coolly, evenly – as if Leo would regret attempting to. Leo rejected it as part of the performance. He left him on the patio and made his way back into the house. The smell of meat cooking was thick in the air and he glanced into the kitchen as he passed down the hallway. Perfecta and Toby were there and looked up from where they were serving green vegetables onto the row of plates on the breakfast counter.

'You leaving us?' Toby seemed genuinely mortified and the look on Perfecta's face said the same.

Leo didn't reply, just made his way to the front door, opened it and walked out into the street. He'd seen enough. Nobody followed.

\* \* \*

'You trying to get an outside line?' The wavering voice of the old boy who'd carried Leo's cases to his room cut in. It appeared he was the receptionist of Hotel L'agneau as well as the bellhop.

'Yes, it's a mobile number.'

'Just press 8 and wait for the dial tone, sir.'

'Thank you.' Leo did as instructed and waited for a reply. He'd left the bathroom mid-shower and was still dripping wet with a towel around his waist. He'd already made two similar trips to the telephone but had second thoughts and hung up. Now it was ringing.

'Hello,' Bookwalter oozed.

'It's Leo.'

'Hey, Leo...you left in quite a hurry.'

'Apologies for that, I just needed some time to take things in. Mull them over.' His nostrils picked up the smell of stale beer and urine wafting through the window.

'Perfectly understandable.' Bookwalter left the line static between them.

'I'd like to take another look at the contract.' Leo felt droplets running cold down his back.

'Of course.' Leo imagined Bookwalter biting his moustache 'Swing by and you can take as long as you want.'

'No. There are a few conditions before I sign and I want to address them to you and your family.'

There was a pause. 'Sure.' It was the last thing he sounded.

'Let me buy you all lunch tomorrow. What was the name of the place you mentioned today?'

'King Crawdaddy's but it's really not necessary.'

'I'm going to fly back tomorrow evening so I'd like to experience some authentic cooking before I leave. One o'clock sound OK?'

'Appreciate that but Perfecta's more than capable of cooking for us.'

'I'm sure but I've already ruined one of her dinners. It would be my way of apologising.'

Another pause. 'OK. Can I ask – why the sudden turnaround?'

'I've been thinking about what you said. I'm

not saying I'm going to sign but I'd at least like the opportunity to look over your figures.'

'I don't think you'll find any fault with those.' Bookwalter's voice became animated again but suspicion still lurked behind it.

'See you all at one then?'

'Wednesday is Perfecta's shopping day and Toby had golf plans. Can we not come to an arrangement between ourselves?'

'That's the condition.' It was Leo's turn to let the line buzz.

'OK. I don't know why you would insist on that if there weren't some ulterior agenda...'

'They're all involved in this. They all benefit from Laura's disappearance. I want them to fully appreciate what it will mean for me to sign this.'

'OK, they'll be there,' Bookwalter chimed in quickly as soon as Leo mentioned his signature.

'One o'clock tomorrow then. I'll make the reservation under my name.'

\* \* \*

Leo rose the next morning as soon as it was light, did the small amount of packing that was necessary and checked out. The old boy said it was fine by him to leave his suitcase behind reception so Leo helped him put it there and walked into town.

It was a cool, grey day and hangers-on seeing out the last days of their vacation filled up the street cafes with their wan expressions. The whole city seemed to need an Alker-Seltzer and Leo's appetite was as absent as everyone else's. He'd made the reservation at King Crawdaddy's the night before when he came across it by chance. He glanced at his watch and realised he still had five whole hours before the Bookwalter family would turn up.

He weaved his way through back streets to the river and, after walking some way along the west bank, he bought a cup of gritty coffee from a snack stand. It looked as if the owner had scooped it out of the Mississippi. The sun came out and tourists on a paddle steamer churned slowly past.

What about Mutatkar? What about the phone call and the room and the laptop? With the Doctor dead, however, Leo suspected he'd probably never find out why he'd contacted him. Dakini Mutatkar knew nothing and Leo had already had his chance to search for any sign of Laura amongst the little the doctor had left behind in Bell Terrace. Maybe it was time to give the laptop and the keys to the police. That prospect seemed even more of a dead end though.

He slung his empty cup into a nearby bin and looked around as if he'd suddenly woken there. How far had he walked? He glanced at his watch again and made his way back to the street to call a cab.

He got it to drop him a couple of streets away from Bookwalter's home and retreated to a combined mini mart and coffee house, nursing several more cups while he waited for lunchtime.

He estimated Bookwalter would leave at about quarter to one to make it to King Crawdaddy's in time but didn't venture near the property until just past the hour. Allowing for the time it would take the family to arrive, get seated, slowly realise he wasn't coming and then drive back home Leo reckoned he had at least three quarters of an hour. A group of kids were playing at the front of the row but didn't pay attention to him as he walked nonchalantly past them and round to the side alley of Bookwalter's place.

# Chapter 22

The sidewall was long and only the far segment of it accounted for the oriental garden. The first segment would be the front room and the kitchen but it was the small bit in the middle that Leo was keen to explore.

To his left were the windows of the next row of houses and Leo hoped that its occupants would be at work. Dead grass and cat urine pinched his nostrils and his temples and stomach buzzed from the overdose of caffeine.

When he reached the end of the wall he could hear the water wheel in the koi pond. He put his hands along the edge of the wall and tensed muscles he hadn't used for some time to pull himself up. Shakily, he rested his knees on the sharp top edge of the wall and looked into the garden and then up to the windows at the back. The panes were dark and gave nothing away so he quickly lifted his legs over the wall and dropped down onto the gravel. He waited for the sound of human alarm from behind him but could only hear the faint shouts of the kids playing at the front. Bookwalter didn't appear to have any sort of security system that Leo had noticed.

Two things had convinced Leo on this course of action. The way Bookwalter's eyes had slipped sideways when they were having their conversation in the garden about what he had that Leo wanted and the five dinner plates that had been lined up on the breakfast bar when he'd left. Leo, Bookwalter, Perfecta and Toby – who had the fifth dinner plate been for?

He followed the wall that he'd just climbed until he reached the area that Bookwalter had glanced at. There was a room, maybe a utility room, with no windows, behind the kitchen. Only a blue-wash painted, wooden door accounted for its presence and a string of weathered red, paper Chinese lanterns hung across it. The room could obviously be accessed through a door at the back of the kitchen but Leo was hoping that he might be able to unlock it from the garden side.

He squeezed on the latch of the door and disappointingly found it didn't budge. Then he heard a sound from within. It was a small, barely discernible scrape – metal against concrete – but a reflex made him step away from it and he prepared himself for a scrabble over the wall. He stood and waited, his temples inflating as he felt his circulation suddenly pumping solid in his wrists. He put his thumb on the catch again and pressed slowly down. It stuck solid and his breath snagged in his throat as he waited for it to trigger the noise again. There was nothing this time.

He became suddenly conscious of the water burbling behind him and looked up at the black windowpanes. He put his ear gently to the door and listened but the solid wood was only a sounding board for the blood surging in his head.

Perhaps it had been nothing more than the sound of the lock grating as he'd depressed it. He shifted his ear from the door and stood holding his breath until the back of his brain started to pound. He heard it again – a small scrape and this time he was nowhere near the door. He extended his hand to the latch again but it snapped up before he could touch it. Somebody was opening the door from within. He looked around the garden but there was nowhere to hide himself unless he jumped in the pool. There wasn't even time to cover that distance though so instead he pressed himself against the wall.

The door opened, concealing his hiding place and he heard a step forward. Whoever it was stood at the threshold and Leo could hear them breathing through the open crack. It sounded laboured, like the air was being drawn though something that covered their mouth. They were obviously scanning the garden. Leo realised he still hadn't breathed himself.

Something was about to give but he was afraid even to draw a little air through his nostrils because he knew his lungs would greedily suck in what they needed before he passed out. The other sounds of the garden seemed to recede and the strained breathing of the figure in the doorway slowed. But there was another noise behind it – a low murmuring. Suddenly the door banged shut again and the sound was like a spike in his chest. He gulped some oxygen and felt his heart fluctuate.

He leant forward, put his hands against his knees and felt a warm rush to his head. There was a pile of cigarette butts around his feet and each one was stained with lipstick. His trespass was immaterial – seeing what he suspected he'd find in the room was all that mattered now. He drew some more air in through his nostrils and yanked the door open.

Even though a single light bulb hung down to illuminate the interior, his eyes took a moment to adjust to the contrast between outside and the dinginess within. However, he immediately picked up the glare from the TV screen. It was positioned behind a tiny camera attached to a tripod that pointed in the direction of the back wall. Someone moved there and his eyes quickly adapted in time to register that it was the female in the boiler suit with the shaved head.

She was tied to the chair and a large piece of black tape covered the bottom half of her face. It started to configure itself in the gloom and he could hear her breathing erratically through the tape. He heard the metal scrape as her chair slid back from him along the concrete floor and his eyes darted from her momentarily as he sought other occupants. She was alone.

The feet of her chair struck the back wall as his eyes darted back to her and a muffled exclamation bubbled up behind her gag. Her eyes expanded in panic and he raised his hand to placate her as he squinted through the gloom. He could smell her occupancy of the room; the stale air heavy with breath, perfume and body odour.

It couldn't be Laura. How could she possibly be here? But Leo still couldn't help himself from searching the emaciated features in front of him as he moved further into the room. He realised she probably couldn't see his face, that he was just a black figure in a doorway of light.

She pumped her arms and suddenly she was free from her bonds and on her feet. Her hand went to her mouth and Leo heard a painful rip as she tore the tape from her face.

'Who the fuck are you?' Her voice and her face confirmed what he suspected and splintered the moment he wanted to believe. She wasn't from Louisiana but her American accent was as unfamiliar as the bottom half of her features. Her mouth solidified around the end of her question, lips pursing around bad teeth.

'John asked me to call in and check on you. See if there was anything you needed.' He watched her shoulders sag in relief.

'Are we off line then?'

'Yeah, just time for a cigarette break.'

'I thought you was an intruder...Jesus.' She sat back down on the chair and put her head briefly in her hands. She ran her green varnished fingertips over the faint spikes on her head and stood again, pulling a pack of cigarettes out of the breast pocket of the boiler suit. 'When am I going to get cable out here?' She pushed past him and he wondered if she was even in her twenties.

He looked at the ropes on the chair that had been knotted so she could slip out of them when necessary and at the TV positioned behind the camera, beyond the vision of anyone logging on. He followed her out and found her sitting on the edge of the pool with her bare feet dangling in the water.

'Know I've been told to stay out of the house but I'm ·ving to pee. I hope he's stocked up the refrigerator.'

he was very young – probably seventeen. 'Tell him I can't survive on Sprite and Lunchables. Not when he's only paying me twenty bucks an hour.' She dragged her feet out of the water and strode off in the baggy boiler suit to open the back door. She tried the handle and it didn't budge. 'Hey, how did you get in?'

'Over the wall. John didn't give me a key.'

She seemed to accept this and produced a few keys from her pocket. 'How long have I got?'

Leo looked at his watch. 'Server's down. Knock yourself out.'

'You gonna tell if I use his jacuzzi?'

'Your secret's safe with me.' He watched her disappear inside and considered following her to exact a bit of damage in Toby's bedroom. The idea of trashing a teenager's computer seemed pitiable though. Distancing himself from Bookwalter and his reprehensible enterprise seemed to be the best way to make himself feel better about ever having become associated with him in the first place.

Before he pulled himself back over the wall, however, he dumped the webcam and its tripod into the swimming pool.

Leo had booked his own flight for nine that evening so returned to L'agneau and slept properly for a couple of hours for the first time in days. He awoke in plenty of time to make it to the airport, splashed his face with water and headed down to reception to pick up his bag just before seven. The old boy at reception seemed relieved to see him.

'Mr Sharpe, I didn't know you were here. Agnes thought you'd walked off with the key but I told her you wouldn't – not while we still had your bag in back.'

'I'm sorry. There was nobody around when I came back. I wasn't sure if I had to check out at a certain time or if it was OK for me to use the room til my flight.'

'Check out's at midday so I'm gonna have to charge you for an extra day.'

'O...K.' Leo pulled out his wallet and extracted his credit card.

'Been serving at the private bar all afternoon.'

'That's probably why I missed you.'

'Usually it's just for guests but as he was waiting on you... Wish I'd known you'd gone up to your room. I could have told him.'

'Sorry. Who?'

'Gentleman that's been waiting on you. I'll go tell him. He's just called a cab...ah...'

Leo turned in the direction of the old boy's gaze and found Bookwalter standing in the doorway of the lounge bar.

# CHAPTER 23

'Your friend's returned,' the old-timer said jovially to Bookwalter.

'So I see...' Bookwalter's matching khaki shorts and shirt were unkempt, his expression unreadable. 'We all missed you today, Leo.'

'How did you know I was staying here? You followed me from the airport, didn't you?'

Bookwalter's hurt frown looked genuine. 'Just hit recall when we got back from the restaurant. Spoke to this gentleman and he said I could come here and wait on you.'

Leo was about to turn in the direction of the old boy but knew his features would confirm this.

'He tells me you're leaving?' Bookwalter wiped the edges of his moustache with his thumb and forefinger.

Leo did turn to the hotelkeeper this time and his wizened features looked uneasy.

'If you had second thoughts about signing you should-d talked to me,' Bookwalter slurred. He was drunk and Leo wondered how long he had been waiting for him in the private bar while he slept upstairs.

Leo didn't look at Bookwalter but sensed him move a step forwards. 'Nothing else to discuss. My flight is in a few hours. Could I have my case, please?'

The old boy nodded emphatically, eager to have any unpleasantness over and done with. He disappeared into the small room behind reception and Leo heard Bookwalter taking another faltering shuffle forward. He'd obviously let go of the doorframe.

'Nothing else to discuss? There is the small matter of you break-er-ing and entering.'

Leo had hoped his trespass wouldn't be discovered before he left but now it seemed that telling Bookwalter what he'd found would be the perfect way to break off any further dialogue. 'Twenty dollars an hour and all the TV you can watch – you'll never be short of Lauras.'

'You had no right to enter my property.'

'I just climbed the wall.'

'No matter. I'm going to have you arrested here and now.'

'Don't be ridiculous.' Leo smelt Bookwalter's parmesan breath as he slopped forward in his flip-flops and picked up the telephone.

Bookwalter dialled. 'Set up a fake business meeting so you could ransack my home.' It was the first time Leo had heard genuine anger in his voice.

'I didn't ransack your home. I didn't even go inside it.'

'No. I've got a witness who'll swear to it that you did though. Linnea would do anything for a few extra bucks and I can have the place trashed before the police get there.'

Leo met Bookwalter's skewed gaze. He didn't doubt that a venal teenager prepared to be tied to a chair for hours on end wouldn't object to earning such easy money. 'Go home and sleep it off.'

'If they don't arrest you here they can catch up with you at the airport. Could be a long time before you get home.' Bookwalter's squint seemed more pronounced and he narrowed his other eye while he waited for a reply.

'Why are you doing this? This is over.'

'Police. Yes, I want to report a break-in.'

Leo cut the call with his finger. 'Enough. Go home to your family.'

'Half an hour of your time.' Bookwalter didn't meet his eye and started dialling again.

Leo sighed. 'What for?'

'Just half an hour and I'll drop the charges. Refuse and I'll finish making this call when you leave.'

'You can't make any more money from Laura or me.

211

What else is there left to discuss?'

'This isn't business, this is about me. Half an hour on the way to the airport – I'll drop the charges and be out of your life.'

The old boy returned with Leo's case.

'Cab for Bookwalter,' a female voice croaked.

The three of them turned in the direction of the entrance where a harassed woman with messy straw-blonde hair stood.

The old boy had been relieved that the three of them left together and after their cab driver had insisted on lugging Leo's case and securing it in the car, Bookwalter climbed into the front.

'Armstrong International via Claiborne Avenue.' Bookwalter slammed his door.

Leo hadn't even closed his before the cab took off and suddenly he had the sensation that he was relinquishing control over events. 'So, where are we going first?'

'I'll spring for the cab fare. If this lady wouldn't mind waiting while we stop off.'

'No problem, hon.' Her meter accelerated faster than she did so she sounded more than happy with the arrangement.

The sky was overcast but it was still close and the aircon blew her stale perfume and Bookwalter's breath into Leo's face.

'What time is the flight?' Bookwalter tried to turn

in his seat but only got his head halfway round.

'We should have time.' Why the hell had he agreed to this? He hadn't really taken Bookwalter's drunken threat seriously. Perhaps he really did need to satisfy his curiosity before he left. Despite his selective psychosis, Leo couldn't deny that he was perversely fascinated by Bookwalter and morbidly inquisitive as to what his last desperate manoeuvre would be. Was he now dispensing with the notion that Bookwalter could be dangerous though?

Nothing he'd seen had persuaded him that he was capable of anything more than cryptic but meaningless internet dialogue and inflated theatrics. However, as they were now heading for an unknown location, which would have set off alarm bells before his discovery of the self-incarcerated Linnea, he wondered if relaxing his guard was exactly what Bookwalter wanted.

Leo leant forward. 'What's in Claiborne Avenue?'

'We're going just off of it.' Bookwalter pointed a pudgy finger at the car radio. 'Mind if I turn that up?'

The three of them spent the rest of the short journey in the company of some middle-of-the-road rock channel that both Bookwalter and the cab driver seemed to enjoy before the cab slowed down and turned into Claiborne Avenue.

'Just over there.' Bookwalter stabbed a finger at the open gates of a cemetery.

The cab driver turned to look at Bookwalter. 'You sure, hon?'

'It's still early. We should be OK. You all right to wait?'

'It's your money. Half hour tops, though.' She pulled the cab in front of the gates and switched off the engine.

Bookwalter got out of the car and Leo followed. His host flip-flopped unsteadily to the gates without waiting for him. Leo had heard how the cemeteries in New Orleans were rife with muggers and dealers but said nothing as they walked inside.

'Everybody's buried above ground here. Katrina caused some minor flooding but the tombs were virtually untouched when the waters soaked away.'

Leo could see a muddy brown waterline at the same height on the rows of mausoleum-type structures that bordered the pathway. Most of them looked dilapidated; their slated roofs crumbling and sprouting tufts of green grass through gaping cracks.

'Do you like jazz?' Bookwalter stopped and turned briefly but only, it appeared, to solicit a response so he knew Leo was still with him.

'No.'

'Lot of famous musical artists are buried here. Danny Barker, Ernie K Doe...' Bookwalter wobbled forward again.

'So...is this a musical pilgrimage?'

Leo didn't like Bookwalter's lack of response and as they turned the corner into another row he looked back at the cab as it disappeared from sight. They continued in silence for a while, the only sound Bookwalter's flip-flops and the occasional pocket of air getting trapped in his sinuses.

The gated tombs seemed to have been forgotten, dead yellow blooms curling from their pots behind fences bloated with rust. The sky threatened rain and it looked like the hungover city was going to get the cleansing it desperately needed.

He caught sight of somebody moving between the adjacent rows to his right but the figure was gone before he could glimpse it properly. Somebody whistled way off and the echo of two dogs fighting increased his feeling of unease.

'How much further do we have to go?'

'I'm not really sure,' Bookwalter drawled blithely.

He had one more minute and then Leo was turning back in the direction from which they'd come. Bookwalter took a wide arc down another row and headed towards a crossroads of ornate tombs. The largest one had a toppled cross on its roof and in front of them on the path, a stone urn had been smashed. Bookwalter stopped and appeared to be getting his bearings.

'Look...I don't want to miss this flight.'

'I'll pay for a later one if... It's OK, I think we're here.' Bookwalter slopped purposefully forward, stepping onto the sepia grass and weaving his way around the back of the tomb with the toppled cross.

Leo followed tentatively and found Bookwalter breathing hard in a small square patch of dirt formed by the backs of four tombs. The suddenly enclosed space made Bookwalter's breath bounce from every side. Leo heard his own swallow echo back at him as he waited for an explanation.

Bookwalter appeared to be gathering himself. To focus, gird or just for effect Leo couldn't say. 'Ever get sick of inhabiting yourself?' The short journey had obviously taken it out of Bookwalter and he breathed in close and heavy behind the words.

'What do you mean?' But he knew exactly what he meant.

'They say that a high proportion of serial killers are in their thirties because they've reached a common crisis point.' Bookwalter seemed to be concentrating on getting the words out whole. 'Their lives haven't panned out and they need to shake things up – to become more significant than they are through any means. Combine that with the sort of mind-numbing job that allows too much time to think – to obsess – and it's small wonder serial killing's not a more common pre-cursor to midlife crisis.'

'And that's why you confessed to being the Vacation Killer.' Leo looked at his watch but didn't register the time.

'No, that's when I came here. Used to be my late-night haunt. Booze and bad company were nev-very-welcome with Jean.'

Bookwalter's first reference to what Leo assumed was his ex-wife seemed to hint at something more than another elaborate con and he waited for the smudgy narration to continue.

Bookwalter breathed in some parched air through his nostrils. 'I wasted a lot of time here – drunk, stoned, paying for what I never got at home – but I can't say that I've ever really regretted it. I needed-do it before I could get myself straight.'

Was this just going to be an indulgent outpouring? He supposed that Bookwalter's Christian sensibility had to have an outlet for guilt but was he really trying to justify himself to Leo in the final few minutes before he left?

'She was face down in that corner when I stabbed her.'

# CHAPTER 24

Leo looked at Bookwalter's profile. He was biting his moustache and looking at the area of dirt in the right-hand corner of where they stood. 'Who?' He tried to imbue the word with weary scepticism but failed.

'I don't know.' Bookwalter shuffled forward and looked at the patch of ground as if it might yield an answer. 'She told me her name was Candy but that was probably false.'

More carefully rehearsed histrionics? Leo studied Bookwalter's reflective expression and told himself that it couldn't be anything else.

'Picked her up in Tooley's Bar and Grill. Think she was new to the streets. She was with some older junkie whore who couldn't wait to palm her off on me.'

Leo suddenly imagined being at home with

Bookwalter's words rattling across his screen. He seemed to be telling the story in the same style he'd spun his account of kidnapping Laura from Chevalier's.

'I'd been thinking about killing for months before that but not that evening. Then she'd shown me her switchblade. One of her tricks had given it to her. In lieu of service I guess. She showed it to me with her black chipped nails.' Bookwalter clenched both his hands a few times and then scratched his knee.

Leo found himself registering the four possible exits from where they stood but still felt incredulity ballooning in his throat. 'Why is it so important you tell me this?'

'I want to put myself in context.'

Leo snorted derision involuntarily. The sound reverberated and Bookwalter looked around as if he didn't know where the noise came from before fixing Leo with a drunk and blankly ingenuous expression. It was Leo's turn to look at the patch of earth.

'She actually let me tie her up here. Thought I was kinky. We hadn't even agreed on a price.' He swallowed. 'She had her whole life in front of her but she'd already thrown it away.'

'So you killed her...there.' Leo pointed and accelerated the story. Whether it was to hasten his exit from the cemetery and being in his narrator's company or because it was starting to make him feel uneasy he didn't know.

'No. I don't think I killed her. I stuck the blade into her five or six times while she lay face down; actually felt the metal scrape against her spine when I pulled it out. Then she did something that genuinely unnerved me.'

And Leo knew exactly what it was.

'I don't know whether it was a reflex or if it was her being guileful, but she raised her tied hands as I knifed her and when I tried to push them down she curled her fingers around the tops of mine. She didn't grab them, she seemed to caress the three fingers of my right hand...stroked them...and I remember how it had taken me out of the moment. It unnerved me and I remember slapping her hand away and stabbing her again.'

Leo didn't look up from the dirt. Hearing Bookwalter replicate the specific details that he'd used describing his abduction of Laura made him remember how convincing they'd seemed when he read them over and over on his laptop. It always seemed that they had been cut and pasted from a real experience and it now appeared that Bookwalter had inadvertently revealed their origin. Or was that what he wanted Leo to believe?

'Is this another ploy?' He still didn't look up from the dirt.

'I came back here about a week later.' He appeared not to have heard and it was like his reaction to the other occasions Leo had attempted to interrupt his online reminiscences. 'There'd been nothing on the TV or in the papers. There was no body here. She'd either crawled away or somebody had found her and taken her...maybe to do something a lot worse than I did. I waited for weeks. After months I gave up on her.' Bookwalter seemed genuinely crestfallen.

Leo resisted the urge to believe the story. It seemed such an unexceptional account in comparison to his more egotistic narration that it immediately appeared true, but that was what Bookwalter did best. That was why Leo was standing in a cemetery in New Orleans.

'Then I hooked up with Coker. I met him through a chatroom and we seemed to have a lot of common interests. He and I formed our own discussion group – the Toolbox Forum. Coker was an IT wizard on the side, everything was password protected and open only to a handful of select members.'

Leo had forgotten his watch and listened. Whether it had been carefully rehearsed or not, Bookwalter definitely seemed to be heading towards something significant.

'It was an ideas exchange. I think the other guys were just getting their rocks off but Coker was earnest. Cocksucker.'

It was the first time Leo had ever heard Bookwalter resort to obscenity and it shocked him to hear it.

'One time I logged onto the forum and Coker was the only other online. He was always online. Took his laptop wherever he was staying. We started talking about the Interstate Strangler.' Bookwalter squinted at Leo expecting recognition.

Leo pursed his lip and shook his head.

'Edward Sloman. He'd been arrested a couple of days before. He'd murdered eight prostitutes between Waynesboro and Charlottesville after picking them up, giving them spiked alcohol and choking them to death in motels while they were still unconscious.' Bookwalter reeled off the details like a mantra. 'Sloman actually wanted to be caught but Coker and I got talking about his method and how it could be expanded on. Coker was a sensationalist, liked the idea of unsolved, high-profile homicide. He came up with the concept of murdering someone in every US state using a unique method, which could only be attributed to him. He travelled around a lot so I could see why the idea excited him. Then I trumped his ace and said wouldn't it be more effective to murder internationally. That really popped his corn. Cocksucker.'

Leo watched Bookwalter's spittle spray onto the dirt and his body stagger slightly sideways before he righted himself.

'I actually came up with the name Vacation Killer during that discussion. And it was me who thought of removing the jawbone, boiling it and posting it to the police wrapped in an item of the victim's clothing. Coker thought I was just an amateur, a fantasist. Didn't believe me when I told him what I did here.'

Leo visualised Bookwalter crouching in the dirt with the girl face down.

'I knew he was a killer for real though. I knew that because he never talked about himself like the others. There was no boast in him. It was like he was gathering data, always pumping everybody, pushing them to open up.'

Either Bookwalter was telling the truth or it was his best performance yet, but Leo could think of no reason for him to denigrate himself like this. It was a far cry from the claims he'd adhered to during the months of their exchanges, and trying to desperately associate himself with some other online sociopath seemed to be the ultimate illustration that nothing he'd ever said until now was true.

'I even swapped ideas with Coker about the random emails. He liked the idea of sending them to advertise his crimes to unconnected parties before the bodies were found but it was me that suggested spamming organisations with details of potential victims before they'd been murdered.' Bookwalter's mortification was apparent. 'I also had the idea to arrange the internal organs of victims like a clock face and use the arms as minute and hour hands – he never took that up.'

'So you know exactly who the Vacation Killer is but you've never told anybody.'

'I'm the Vacation Killer.' Bookwalter's voice was suddenly level again as if he'd realised he'd said too much and was trying to rein himself in. 'Coker may have sent the emails and murdered the girls but he was a charlatan with no imagination. I've told you, the trick is to refuse amateurs like him oxygen.'

If there had been any conflict left in Leo about whether Bookwalter's insanity was selective, it had now evaporated. His admission to playing second fiddle to Coker, but having concealed this fact to spare his own warped ego, dispensed with the idea that he was nothing more than an astute businessman.

'After that conversation I never heard from him again. I tried to re-establish contact when the first victim of the Vacation Killer hit the news and the emails started circulating but he refused to speak to me. I wondered if he'd get in touch when I set up the website but it looks like he's happy to remain anonymous.'

Leo tried to process the implications of what he was saying and imagined fingernails other than Laura's caressing the murdering hands that hung at Bookwalter's sides. 'So Coker goes unpunished, you get to earn a few bucks and Bonsignore takes the glory from both of you to the grave.'

Bookwalter's frame seemed to tense at the mention of the name and the trapped spark of vitriol suddenly energised his lips. 'Bonsignore is irrelevant. There were plenty of people who tried to claim responsibility for the Vacation Killings. The police decided to believe Bonsignore because they were desperate and he worked for the same feed company as Coker.' His mouth snapped shut again as did his left eye; he had said too much again. He closed his other eye for a moment as if summoning a reserve of patience. 'I'm telling you these things in confidence, Leo. I'm telling you these things because I want you to understand who I am.' His tone was overly amicable and they both knew he'd revealed more than he wanted to.

'I'm leaving.' It seemed like the only course of action to Leo. He backed away a couple of paces and was just preparing to turn the corner of the tomb. The quicker he blocked Bookwalter from sight the better.

'Wait. The photo of your wife. Don't you want to know who gave it to me?'

Leo paused and glimpsed the desperation in Bookwalter's squinted features. 'Who?'

'Sign the disclaimer and I'll tell you.'

Leo shook his head. 'Jesus.' He turned and walked away from Bookwalter's killing ground. For a while all he could hear was the sound of his own footsteps on the path then he heard movement behind him. He turned. Bookwalter was still out of sight but the sound of his flip-flops indicated he was coming closer. Leo turned and strode faster.

'Your sister-in-law, Ashley Pritchett, she gave them to me!'

His voice was far enough behind him to resist the temptation to run. It appeared Bookwalter wanted the last word, to play a surprise hand. He had. But Leo kept walking and didn't look back even after he'd got into the cab.

# CHAPTER 25

?

It was all the response Leo needed to justify the cancellation of his flight back to the UK. He sat back in his uncomfortable plastic silver chair, his morning coffee suddenly tasting bitter on his tongue.

Apart from a Japanese couple seated at the computer to his right, the internet café was empty. Even though the aircon cooled his face from the grill above, his nostrils still couldn't escape the smell of the remains of Mardi Gras rotting.

Was this just a ploy so he wouldn't have to return to his non-existence in the UK...to Ashley? No, this was significant enough to legitimise delaying that particular confrontation. Forget the anonymity of cyberspace, nobody, it appeared, was exactly who he'd thought they were – Matty, Ashley, even Laura had concealed things from him. Laura had done it for all the right reasons, and he was hoping that Ashley would have similar grounds, but Leo couldn't help feeling that things had been deliberately kept from him, things he should have been part of.

He looked at the question mark and tried to imagine the finger that had typed it, and then the body it was connected to, and the blank face that resided between its shoulders. The email reply had been almost immediate as if it had responded to his internal dialogue.

*If he replies then Laura is alive.*

He'd logged onto the Gristex website without really expecting it to lead him anywhere or knowing what to do to begin his search. But when he'd clicked through to the contact page he'd noticed that the list of names for the myriad agricultural departments consisted of email addresses that simply used surname and number before the company name: palmer56@Gristex.com etc. If it *was* his real name, how many Cokers were likely to be working for them? He opened his mail and composed an email to: coker@Gristex.com.

He then sent the same email to Cokers 1, 2, 3 and 4 and stopped at 5 when all but the first Coker email was returned unsent. So, only one Coker working for Gristex.

*Dear Mr Coker,*

*howdy doody,*

*heard you knew my wife*

*tall, freckle faced, chicken pox scar*

*reply as soon as you get this*

*you probably won't want to forward it*

Leo had just been about to close down his email when the reply had appeared in his inbox.

*?*

One Mr Coker working for Gristex.

\* \* \*

Gristex Cattle Feed Products had headquarters in most states but its main production, sales and distribution nucleus operated out of Montana. That was where Coker was. It seemed preposterous that a man who had very probably committed the sadistic crimes that Bonsignore had confessed to, continued his daily, nine-to-five existence purely because of Bookwalter's vanity.

Leo's first reflex was to inform the police – let them take Bookwalter into custody and tell them about his internet dialogues with Coker. When they knew that Coker worked for Gristex – probably knew Bonsignore if he shared a similar work itinerary – they would surely have to reopen the investigation. But when Leo considered Bonsignore's stance for the months he'd been in prison, he knew that it was likely that Coker could remain just as silent about the whereabouts of his victims. Locked away, what good was he to Leo? It could be the start of the same waiting process, even if he was the real Vacation Killer.

Leo made up his mind about travelling to Petroleum County before he'd even come to this conclusion, however. He'd never suspected that accepting Bookwalter's invitation could have led to anything more than a final confirmation of his fraudulence but, as he was already in the States, finding Coker could now be his only course of action.

He didn't send another email to Coker and figured the one he'd sent would have made him sufficiently uneasy. After closing his email account, he took a cab directly to the airport and booked a flight to Billings Logan International Airport. Gristex's hometown of Winnett was approximately eighty miles drive from there and he used his waiting time to hire a car and book a room at the only hotel in town.

Winnett was certainly a different scene to New Orleans. Surrounded by flat farm country, most of which was privately owned by ranchers, the town consisted of about three hundred white people living in half the amount of houses. It had seen its gas and oil boom days in the fifties and sixties, but now the previous population of two thousand had depleted, and many of the buildings were just empty shells.

The town itself nestled in a valley, the white-painted houses in stark contrast to the towering, square-topped mountains that surrounded them. A wonky white 'W' was painted along the bluff but it didn't feel like the sort of place that really wanted to advertise itself. And after passing several hand-made anti-meth campaign placards Leo began to get an idea of what living in this sort of remoteness could do to a person.

He pulled up at the Kozy Korner Café and Bar, realised how hungry he wasn't and gunned the engine of the unwieldy, black Chevy Suburban he'd picked up at the airport. He'd felt invincible sitting within it, protected from the green but dusty terrain, but there really had been very few chances for him to collide with any other vehicles.

It didn't take him long to find the only hotel in Winnett. The Montana Rest Stop Hotel looked more like a large garage, and he looked up and sighed at its weathered white frontage before opening the car door and climbing down from the driver's seat. It was mid-morning but the sun already felt blistering on his scalp.

He was pleasantly surprised by the smart tiled lobby with a piano in the corner – it felt homely. A shy girl with pink hair in braids, who couldn't have been more than seventeen, signed him in. She told him it was a communal bathroom and that he'd have no TV, but her enthusiasm made them sound like amenities to be proud of. She appeared to have no local accent, something he'd noticed of everyone he'd been in contact with since he'd touched down. Coming from New Orleans the absence was conspicuous.

He dumped his bag on the bed and wondered if there was any reason to delay his visit to Gristex. Its headquarters were about five miles out of town near the Musselshell River and he guessed not many people who worked there resided in Winnett. It was such a remote location that Leo wondered what the company had to hide. According to the website it was entirely self-sufficient with a high percentage of its staff living on site. Leo felt alone and utterly disconnected from the UK and saw how people who wanted to hide could deliberately lose themselves in such an otherworldly environment.

His stomach bayed and his legs wobbled from lack of food, but he knew he wouldn't be able to swallow anything until he'd found Coker. He made his way down the landing to the communal bathroom and after wetting his lips carried on down the stairs and back out into the car park, exchanging a nervous smile with the pink-haired girl on the way out.

Gristex's headquarters weren't exactly what Leo expected. Anticipating a shard of polished glass staked into the countryside, he was surprised to find it an unshowy brownstone building, crouched low and flat in the dust, its considerable, two-storey width flattened out along the horizon. He took one of the named parking spaces nearest the front of the building but away from the main entrance. The expansive car park was nearly full to capacity but there was nobody to be seen and a warm breeze blew across the silent, eerie spectacle. As Leo got out of the car and looked back at the rows of cars behind him, he wondered if the approach he'd decided on was still feasible.

# CHAPTER 26

The aggressive aircon in the reception area gave him goosebumps as he stepped in through the immense glass doors. A middle-aged receptionist smiled at him and he walked towards her through the white-washed seating area.

'How can I help you today?' She seemed to expect him to answer the question long before he'd arrived at her leather-fronted station.

Leo smiled as he leant casually on the reception desk. 'I've an appointment with Mr Coker.' Was that a curly blonde wig she was wearing? He tried to focus on her pink-glossed mouth.

'Alrighty.' She nodded and tapped the keyboard to her computer, then frowned. 'And your name is?'

'Geoffrey Chase.' It was the name on the back of a

removals lorry he'd followed out of Winnett.

'There's nothing here.' There was mortification in her voice. 'When did you make the appointment?'

'Only yesterday. Very informally. He said he didn't think it would be a problem.'

'I'll just call him. What's his first name?'

'I have his card here somewhere.' Leo searched through his leather jacket for her benefit and could feel her eyes appraising him.

'Is this work-related?' She didn't sound as if she would believe him if he said it was.

'Kind of. He said he was the only Coker who worked here. Would you have his details there?'

'Let me check.' She tapped at her keyboard again. 'Wesley Coker?'

'That's him,' he said a little too quickly.

'Take a seat and I'll try and search him out.'

Leo sat in the row of matching brown leather seats nearest the reception.

'Hi Jane, it's Margot. I've got a Mr Chase here. Australian I think. Has an appointment with Mr Coker but I've got nothing on my spreadsheet…OK. Thanks, Jane. Are you going to the factory cook-out tonight? Yeah, coleslaw duty for me as well. No, the band's cancelled so you know what that means. We'll be leaving long before the line-dancing though. OK. See you there.' The receptionist replaced the phone. 'Mr Coker's just coming out of a meeting so he'll be down right now.'

'Thanks.' Leo half stood to receive the news, sat again, waited for a few moments and then stood and walked back to reception. 'Just remembered I've left something in my car. Be two minutes.'

'OK, Mr Chase.' She seemed eager to show him she'd remembered his name.

Leo strode through the sliding doors again and the heat draped itself back over him. He turned right and walked back to his car, climbing back up into it and sitting back in the driver's seat until his circulation slowed. Then he started the engine and reversed out of the space, manoeuvring it to a parking space behind the front row so he could watch reception.

Margot was talking on the telephone to someone else but Leo kept his focus on the swing doors either side of her. From somewhere in the building, Wesley Coker was on his way to meet him.

A couple of minutes later a tall man appeared through the doors to the left. Leo was expecting another Bookwalter so Coker's androgynous appearance took him by surprise. He wasn't very old, mid to late thirties, with a neatly kept mane of pale blonde hair that came down to his shoulders. His sharp, handsome features were a raw colour, as if he'd been exposed to the cold and his gait was very effete, his loose-fitting white shirt and tan chinos flapping about his slender body.

Leo watched him wait for Margot to finish and then

their brief exchange. Margot gestured towards where Leo had sat and then out of the doors. They both looked outwards and, it seemed, directly at where he was now parked. He studied the acute features of Wesley Coker as his eyes narrowed at the car park. Coker studied his watch before sitting heavily on a seat in the waiting area as if his slight frame were already exhausted with the action of standing up.

Watching Coker, Leo started the engine and quickly reversed out of the space. Margot was back on the telephone and as he spun the wheel and headed down the row the wrong way the movement made Coker turn in his direction. But Leo had already disappeared from sight. So now he'd put a name to a face, what next?

He only had to wait a few moments before the question had been answered. An arrow on a sign at the end of the row pointed right to Gristex Village.

He found a smaller, gravelled car park at the back of a building that served as a forecourt for a similar two-storey conglomeration. The housing complex was squeezed tighter together, brighter coloured curtained windows contrasting with the grey blinds of the main building. There was no human movement, and even though it was likely most of the occupants would be at their desks or working in the factory, it was still eerily quiet. As he crunched over the gravel and then the soft Astroturf verge that led to the homes, however, he

240

began to pick up sounds – a TV or radio somewhere, a baby crying and the low motor hum of some domestic appliance.

His eyes soon adjusted from the glare of the sun to the cool shade of the labyrinth of slim, flagstoned walkways. These narrowly divided the uniform, navy-blue front doors. The whole setting reminded him of the time he and Laura had visited Venice – this was a uniquely detached community that preferred its privacy and isolation.

He stopped at the mailbox of the third residence, set into the wall beside the front door. The name of the occupants was written in a small Perspex window. Thomas Frescabaldi was the occupant of number five. Leo wondered how long it would take him to find Coker. He backtracked and checked that neither of the previous doors belonged to him and then continued down the alleyway.

Turning the corner he ran into a heavily pregnant red-headed woman pushing a pram. She smiled at him through her freckles and they awkwardly negotiated around each other. Leo stepped over the wheels of the pram so she could get by and flattened himself against the wall until she'd passed. He looked back and so did she and he wasn't sure if it was because he was a stranger or because she thought her jagged denim hot pants had done the trick. She was good looking and probably in her late twenties. Had to be a tedious life out here. She half smiled and continued on her way as Leo focused on the next door.

Like Venice he suddenly found himself in a small square with passageways leading off from each corner. Instead of a church or pizzeria however he found himself outside what looked like a community hall. Some sun-faded stars and stripes flags hung along its metal-shuttered facade and a hand-written sign pinned on the door advertised the 'BBQ' that Margot had been discussing. He decided to take the corner immediately in front of him with a payphone beside it.

Minutes later he was lost and couldn't even find his way back to the square. He passed Matthew and Jolie Romero's mailbox for the third time and looked at his watch. It felt like he'd been walking around in there for hours but it had been scarcely thirty minutes. He still had a lot of ground to cover and his circuits of one section were starting to make him anxious. He really should have eaten and he could feel his knees starting to liquefy.

He arrived at a familiar crossroads and turned left this time; positive that he hadn't encountered the names on the mailboxes he passed on the long passageway that led to the next crossroads. Before he turned, however, he found Wesley Coker's name underneath the mailbox of the last house in the row. He stared at it for a moment and then up and down the passage. Nobody was around. Even if anyone did see him Leo wondered if they'd recognise him as an outsider or if the various departments of Gristex were as exclusive to each other as any other organisation.

He peered through the nets of the window over the mailbox and made out daylight through an open doorway at the back of the kitchen. He walked to the end of the crossroads and turned right, finding himself in an open area of compact back gardens. The gated squares of grass in each allotted area looked like Astroturf as well and identical terracotta troughs of cacti were positioned on every back windowsill.

It was to be his second domestic trespass but he doubted that Coker or any of the other residents would have need for heavy security measures in such a remote location. He tried the handle of the frosted glass back door. It didn't budge. Then he noticed the tiny gap between the back downstairs window and the ledge. He could just see the edge of the net curtain undulating in the crack.

'Help you with something?'

Leo turned to find a balding man with a large liver spot at his right temple. He looked to be in his sixties but wore a faded black Dropkick Murphys T-shirt and tracksuit bottoms. He had a bag of shopping in each hand.

Leo thought quickly. 'I'm visiting Wes but he's not home yet.'

The man's pinched leather brown features relaxed a little. 'You related?'

'Sort of.'

'Can't remember the last time he had any visitors. Works too hard. Hope you're going to lead him into mischief – God knows, I've tried. I'm Sam Harlow, my wife died five months ago.'

Sam extended his hand and Leo didn't know how to react. 'Sorry to hear that.' His fingers were being crushed.

'Got a key if you're interested. He left it with me for emergencies and for watering his bonsai when he's on vacation.'

Leo couldn't believe his luck. The crime in this community was probably nil. 'That would be great.'

'One condition. Whatever you plan to do together – count me in.'

# CHAPTER 27

Leo imagined the average Gristex home would be uniformly soulless but was still taken aback when he entered Coker's home. How long had he worked for the company? Perhaps he'd only just moved in to this particular unit – this seemed to be the only explanation for the scant furnishings within. He guessed that the framed pictures of bloody sunsets that adorned the place were probably hanging in every other house on the block, but the powder terracotta furniture that matched the walls didn't even look as if it had been sat on. The only small area of inhabitation was the 'office' which consisted of a slightly paper-cluttered computer desk in the space under the slatted wooden stairs. He glanced through the small pile of utility bills there and wondered if it was worth turning on the computer.

An electric air freshener hissed peridodically from the corner, leaving a distinct smell of coconut oil in the air. Walking into the small champagne-tiled kitchen, Leo found no dirty dishes or cutlery in the sink and only some meagre staples in the fridge. Coker was clearly a man who took advantage of the staff canteen.

He climbed the stairs to the small landing above and found the main bedroom. A pair of sandals was the only immediate sign of occupation until he slid open the wall-to-ceiling wardrobe door. Crisp pastel shirts, ties and chinos hung on the rack and a small selection of brown leather shoes were neatly arranged below. He opened Coker's bedside drawer and was suddenly assailed with the same feeling he'd had prior to meeting Bookwalter. Was he rummaging through the belongings of an entirely innocent individual? Then he remembered Bookwalter's graveside confession and Leo considered how outwardly harmless appearances could so easily conceal deeds of the past. And why *would* there be any traces of a person's psychosis, particularly in a homogenous place like this?

There were a few canisters of pills and a folded travel alarm clock. Nothing else. He walked past the small bathroom and looked into the box room. It was just big enough for the bench and weights but nothing else hung on the walls. In fact, nothing of Coker's personality was in evidence except for the three aforementioned bonsai trees sitting on the landing windowsill. Perhaps they came with the house as well though, like the cacti outside. He hadn't seen a book or music collection and as he walked back towards the stairs he wondered how a person could occupy such a small space without some of his self rubbing off. Perhaps he only lived here at weekends? Perhaps he had a wife and kids he returned to? There were no photos though, no pictures of anyone anywhere. He appeared to be an entirely blank person.

Leo walked out of the box room and closed the door gingerly behind him – but to his horror a louder sound accompanied it. It was the downstairs front door banging open. Leo felt the air lock in his chest. He heard footsteps and the sound of rustling paper bags. Coker obviously shared the same shopping day as his neighbour. He heard the impact of the bags on the kitchen counter and then keys being thrown into something china.

Whatever movement he made at whatever point, it was going to alarm Coker as soon as he made his presence known. After a moment's hesitation, he decided to tiptoe down the stairs hoping Coker's movements in the kitchen would mask the sound of his descent. They didn't.

Coker immediately appeared at the kitchen doorway clutching a serrated bread knife at ear height. 'What the fuck are you doing in my home?' There didn't appear to be any fear in his face or voice; in fact, his expression told Leo that if he was a burglar, he'd definitely chosen the wrong house.

Leo was still only a third of the way down the stairs and stopped, his palms outstretched. 'Mr Coker?'

Coker's eyes slitted but he took another step forward; his hand rigidly gripping the handle of the knife while his body seemed to dangle about it. 'So you can read my mailbox. Stay where you are while I dial 911 or I'll use this...it's your choice.'

Either adrenaline had taken over or Wesley Coker could completely disguise his fear because Leo couldn't detect a trace of it. But there was something about the threat, the way that it tripped off his tongue and the look of conviction that accompanied it that made Leo immediately regret this method of approach. He had nothing with which to defend himself – except his words. 'I wasn't satisfied with your response to my email so I thought I'd come and meet you in person.'

Something flickered in Coker's eyes and he at least halted his advance. Not that it made any difference. With Coker's gangling height Leo was sure that one bound would enable him to stab Leo in the leg before he could turn.

'I know everything there is to know about you Mr Coker and if you think I came here alone without making provision for this...' The words surprised Leo more than they did Coker but inverting the truth of the situation made his would-be attacker pause for thought.

'You're an intruder in my home. I have every right to defend myself.'

'You read my email...you know who I am.'

'Remind me,' he said eventually, the knife still raised. Leo considered the benign and vacant way Coker had looked in reception.

'Put the knife down, your arm must be aching.' Leo felt his right eyebrow raise as his throat tightened and closed behind the last word.

'I'm good, thanks.' Coker made no move. 'Why don't you tell me what this is all about?' For the first time Leo registered how nasally monotonous Coker's voice was. In contrast to the sharp and red-raw features it was almost as if his voice was being dubbed, the cruel intent on his face completely lost in translation. Only a slight American twang was discernible. 'I'm guessing you're my no-show appointment and you're name isn't Chase.'

'You're still making me uncomfortable.' Leo's eyes darted between the knife blade and Coker's unblinking features.

'I'm making *you* uncomfortable?' Real incredulity registered now and a half smile tugged at the corner of his thin mouth.

'I'm not here to harm you,' Leo continued.

'I know why you're here, Leo. But you're barking

up the wrong tree. I can't tell you where Laura's buried.'

The area between Leo and Coker seemed to shift, like a magnifying glass moving forwards and back. Coker's acknowledgement of his trespass felt like a screw being tightened in his chest bone. For endless months the woman he loved had almost become a fictional character. Now hearing her name uttered by this stranger in this strange place was even more arresting than any of Bookwalter's fabrications.

'You a bunk buddy of Bookwalter's now? Thought it might have been him that sent the email. Whoever did, I knew Bookwalter wouldn't be able to keep his mouth shut forever.' The knife remained stock still in its fitting of balled fingers.

'So you're not about to deny what he told me?' If Coker chose to lunge at him he knew his body wouldn't respond quickly enough.

'We both know about Bookwalter's delusions of grandeur but I'm guessing he's finally convinced you. You're either here for closure or blackmail.'

'Put the knife down.'

'No.'

'Why?'

'Because if you believe what Bookwalter has told you then from my point of view – the Vacation Killer's point of view – killing you would certainly be my only option.' Coker rolled his eyes upwards and blinked a few times, thinking out loud. 'If you've informed third parties about me being the Vacation Killer it's inevitable I'll be going to jail. So, if I'm to be locked up for those murders I may as well be locked up for yours as well. The other alternative is that you're lying to me and operating completely on your own. You're a bereaved husband doing your own investigation in which case it would definitely do me no harm to kill you now. Missed anything?'

Leo knew that even if Coker wasn't the Vacation Killer, he was capable of using the knife he was holding for the purposes he'd threatened. It was the speed of his response and his confident reflex to finding a stranger in his home that convinced him. Anyone else would have panicked before trying to defend himself; Coker seemed to be treating his discovery of Leo as an agreeable bonus.

'Yes, you're missing the fact that it's me here in person and not the police. Perhaps exposing you isn't my intention.'

'Only because you're not a hundred percent sure – Bookwalter's probably told you so many lies you don't know what to believe.'

Leo considered his escape route. He wasn't sure if there was a lock on the box room door or even if he could reach it and close the door in time. That was if Coker didn't slash the tendons on the back of his legs as he turned to run. He tried to remember the layout in Coker's bedroom but couldn't even remember where the window was.

Coker's expression changed to one of mock concern. 'What's the matter? Isn't that what you came for? Track the Vacation Killer to his blue-collar lair and get him to talk about Laura and how he played with her entrails before he took her jawbone off like he did the others. Dissolving the sinew, stripping it, polishing it. Or is it that you think he spared Laura? Or maybe if he didn't that he can still tell you exactly where you can find what's left of her?'

Gratification registered on Coker's features as he saw the anger mushrooming inside Leo. If Leo attacked him then he knew that it would give him perfect justification to do what he wanted with the blade. Coker waited and Leo's anger pounded at the core of his brain. His only option was to turn and run because down the stairs lay only a pool of his blood and a convenient explanation for Coker. He felt the back of his legs tense but had no doubt that Coker would be quick to read his body language.

He was surprised then, when as soon as Coker seemed satisfied that an attack wasn't imminent, his blade hand dropped to his side. 'Like I said though, I can't give you the information that's most vital to you, Leo.' He used his free hand to scratch his temple. 'Fact is, I didn't kill Laura. Fact is, I've never been to the UK. You don't have to believe me but you'd only have to take a peek at my passport upstairs to verify it.' He raised his eyebrows at Leo.

'Bullshit.' But Coker was in complete control of the situation. It looked like he could easily silence Leo so why try to plead innocence from a position of power?

'This is something I couldn't claim responsibility for. Wouldn't make any odds to Bookwalter or Bonsignore – they wouldn't let facts get in the way of them taking the responsibility for somebody else's deeds. I have standards though. I didn't kill your wife, Leo...or Louis Allan-Carlin.'

'Because, of course, you'd tell me if you did.'

Coker sniffed through one nostril. 'I didn't kill any boys in Montenegro either. That was part of Bonsignore's testimony. Maybe he did but the bodies have never been found. Bonsignore's only proven murder was a crime of passion against his boyfriend...I don't think he knew the first thing about selecting a victim. Jill, Estelle, Gillian, Heather, Cody, Dinora...' Coker paused as if the sixth name echoed a romance. '...and Saphira. I was also in Germany the same time as Bonsignore. I met him briefly at the Gristex conference in Freiburg but he was too busy screwing the bellhop to have murdered anyone. I actually shook hands with Bonsignore. I don't think that entitles him to any credit though, do you?'

Leo couldn't process the information that was spilling so freely from Coker. The names, the casual exposure of information about events that he'd spent months analysing and re-analysing.

'I'm not a homophobe, Leo, but Bonsignore did nothing but implicate me in his own messy love life. If it *was* him, then carrying on the work of the Vacation Killer in the UK was commendable, but having done half a job with your wife I'll never understand why he had to obscure the design further by killing Louis Allan-Carlin. That's if he ever did murder him. It's the only question I really would have liked answered but we'll never know now. Bonsignore was certainly more enigmatic in jail than he ever was outside of it. He kept his mouth shut all that time but, of course, he had no option. He didn't know where any of the women he claimed to have murdered were buried. It's his legacy now though.'

Leo doubted that the man standing before him was talking with such candour because it had been locked inside him for so long; rather it was because he was confident that that none of it would be repeated.

'When I heard about the girls in England and the Allan-Carlin's son I knew it was an out. It had got too messy anyway. After Germany I was on Gristex business in Holland and I'd abducted a girl I'd met in Eindhoven. I'd stunned her with a sledge hammer like the others but she still managed to escape from the trunk of my car. So, when I came back to the US and heard about what was going on in the UK I took it as a sign. Then Bookwalter removed me even further. He'd been clogging up my inbox accusing me of plagiarism. He wanted details and I wouldn't give them to him. He threatened blackmail so I stonewalled him. Next thing I know he's punished me by confessing to the murders he thought he should have committed. I always suspected Bookwalter had all the brains but no application.'

Leo suddenly visualised the patch of dirt where Bookwalter murdered the girl with the black chipped nails.

'Then I realised he had no brains at all.'

Leo wiped his right hand down the wall beside the stairs, his fingertips connecting with the edge of the picture frame of the blood-red sunsets. He intended to send it spinning at Coker's face buying himself enough time to make his escape. But it was hanging by a string and as he tried to pull it from the wall, it caught on the nail and bounced back noisily.

Coker didn't flinch. Didn't blink. Leo waited for a reaction but there was none. The only sound was nasal breathing he wasn't sure was his or not. Coker rolled his eyes and walked back into the kitchen. Leo remained where he was, a clear path to the front door before him. Then he heard the TV being switched on. It sounded like the news channel but this quickly changed to saxophone music. The sound changed again and this time it was some sort of sports coverage. The sound of a crowd swelled as Coker turned up the volume. Leo turned and decided to take his chances in the bathroom although he didn't know if there was a window in there either or if it had a lock. But as he turned, fingers curled around his ankle before he'd lifted his foot up the step.

He thrust himself forward, attempting to put as much of his body out of reach but the grip on his ankle tightened. He heard the wooden steps creaking under Coker's weight and the drag on his leg decreasing as he moved over Leo's flattened body. Leo waited for the pierce of the blade but Coker was moving up further and he guessed it was to cut his vocal cords. Coker obviously didn't want to disturb the neighbours and silencing him would be his first priority.

Snared, Leo felt his chin graze the edge of the step below the top one. He thrust out his hands against it and pushed himself back with as much force as he could. His body slid under Coker and he felt his feet connect with his attacker's shins. Leo heard a yelp of pain as they both shuddered down the stairs and then Coker's weight on him as they hit the bottom. He thrashed out his limbs in all directions and pushed back on the heavy bulk with his spine, freeing himself and righting his balance as he staggered up and backwards against the front door. His back connected with its solidity and he straightened his legs and slid himself up it as Coker got from his knees and turned towards him.

Coker didn't straighten, however. The knife was jutting sideways from the left of his ribcage and a new, dark insignia on his white shirt was spreading to match the blood-red paintings on the walls.

# CHAPTER 28

The knife was almost in to the handle and Coker's mouth was open and silently attempting to draw air. He fell backwards and hard against the bottom of the stairs but the impact didn't register. He looked down at the blade handle as if weighing up his chances of survival and curled his fingers around it – not with any intention of trying to pull it out but almost as if he were caressing it. His fingertips were dyed red against the wound and as his heart pumped more blood around the blade it sprayed the front of his chinos. His feet gave way, the bottoms of his heels sliding the hallway carpet away from his body – but Coker's focus was only on the handle. A noise escaped his mouth. Not a yell or a moan but the sound of something inside rupturing – a low hiss and a gurgle that he had no control over.

Opening the door seemed to take minutes as Leo's fingers fumbled with the handle and he anticipated Coker on his back. As soon as he was out of the house and into the pathway at the back of the gardens however, his instinct to run immediately ebbed. Everything seemed so normal again and he couldn't even hear the sound of the TV from within the house. It was uncannily silent and it immediately decelerated him, his speed walk losing pace before he was back in the main passageway.

In the square he used the payphone to call 911. He wondered how long it would take for an ambulance to reach Coker if he wasn't dead already. Leo thought about the sound that Coker had made but felt desensitised to what had just happened. He wouldn't feel the bruising on his ribs and ankle until he was on the plane home. His brain compartmentalised Coker with the knife sticking in him while another instinct took charge and impelled him to get out of Winnett. Out of Winnett and home. There was no reason to remain a second longer here than he had to.

It seemed only a stroke of luck had allowed Leo to escape with his life. He was also convinced that Coker had been telling the truth about Laura and Louis Allan-Carlin. What reason had he to lie?

He vaguely registered a familiar face smiling at him. It was the red-headed pregnant girl he'd seen earlier, but he didn't notice her expression turn to dismay as she looked into his blank stare.

So Leo was no closer to finding Laura but the trip had brought him closer to the truth or, at least, eliminated the most likely candidates. Bonsignore, Bookwalter, Coker – they were names that had no relevance to what had really happened in Chevalier's on that Christmas shopping day. He'd been looking in the wrong direction.

* * *

The chill and wind of London blasted away the dislocation he'd felt about what had happened in Coker's hallway and as he crossed the tarmac towards baggage retrieval a feeling beyond nausea saturated him. It was likely a serial killer lay at the bottom of the stairs in Winnett – stuck with his own blade as he'd attempted to take Leo's life. But the thought of another human being, whoever they were, dying as a result of Leo's actions was something he knew he'd not even begun to contemplate.

He wondered how much evidence he'd left in the house and what he'd touched – the stair, the picture frame, the fridge and the front door handle at the very least. Perhaps the ambulance had arrived in time to save him – in which case, would Coker really want to tell the truth about what had happened? Whatever the outcome, on the flight home Leo had elected to keep an eye on the area's local news via the internet, find out what had happened and decide when was the best time to submit the info he had on Coker to the state police.

Now though, he needed the company of friends – somebody to relay everything that had happened to him since he'd landed in the States.

More than the desire to see Ashley though was an overriding need to know why she had handed over the photo of Laura to Bookwalter. He tried to recall how many times she'd chided him for his internet dialogue with him. Could Bookwalter have been lying to him? It was certainly a possibility, but Bookwalter's confession to murder in the cemetery had been about trying to validate himself with the little truth he had left to offer, his revelation about Ashley a last ditch attempt to prove he had at least a tenuous connection to Laura.

The taxi dropped him off at Ashley's home in Richmond, but he suddenly realised that he had no UK currency in his wallet – only thirty or so dollars. After knocking several times he glanced at his watch for the first time and realised it was just after seven in the morning – far too early for Ashley.

Leo looked up at the curtain of her front bedroom and was relieved to see it part and fall back into place. He saw a light come on through the stained window above the white-panelled front door, and then she was standing in the hallway in a purple satin nightgown, a hand covering her dishevelled hair.

'Leo, where the hell have you been?' Her features were unusually fierce.

'I'm sorry, Ash. I've been away and the cab's just dropped me off from the airport. I don't have any money.'

Wordlessly, Ashley turned on her bare heels and marched back into the hallway. She pulled out a cluster of notes from one of the ornate dresser drawers and strode back to him, handing the cash over without making eye contact.

After he'd paid the driver and dragged his case into the house, he found Ashley in the front lounge. He offered her the change but she didn't register it, pulling her robe tighter around her. He thought she looked so small and vulnerable standing in the middle of the rug amongst the antique furnishings.

'Why didn't you tell me where you were going when you left the message? Where have you been?'

'I've been to the States.'

Her expression froze. 'What the hell for?'

'I went to see Bookwalter.'

'Bookwalter...I thought you'd promised me not to have anything more to do with him.'

'And what about you, Ash? When did you decide not to have anything more to do with him?'

'That bastard.' Ashley sat down on the sofa, her pearl-painted toes dangling off the floor. 'He said everything would be confidential.' The right-hand side of her face suddenly trembled and Leo realised she was holding back tears. He'd never seen Ashley cry before – not even when Laura went missing. She'd always seemed to keep her emotions private and it was the last thing he expected to see. She bowed her head, composing herself behind her curtain of hair. But when she flicked it back again there was still pain in her eyes. 'He duped me... said putting the photo on his site would keep Laura in the public eye.'

'But Bookwalter is a nut job.'

'Which is why you flew thousands of miles to see him?' She looked at Leo for the first time since he'd entered the house, but there was more than recrimination welling there.

'Your words, Ash. It's what you've been telling me all this time.'

'I didn't want you to make the same mistake I did.'

Leo sat on the sofa beside her and looked at the dirty marks his shoes had made on the oatmeal rug. He felt her gaze on the side of his face.

'He told me he could help me. I was just as desperate as you.' Ashley pleaded.

'I don't understand. I've always known he was a liar. Knew nothing he told me about Laura could be true. But he ended up the only person I could talk to about her disappearance. Everyone else wanted me to move on.'

'What happened when you met him?'

'You haven't answered my question. You've never seemed to be in any doubt about his motives. I willingly indulged him because it seemed to be leading me towards the closest thing I'll ever have to an explanation. Why did you ever associate with him?'

'Why d'you think I warned you off? Have you any idea what it was like for me – how irrational I was at that time? Kenton had just left me, Laura disappeared, everything I'd known evaporated in a matter of months.'

Leo turned – her face was only an inch away. There were tears in her eyes and the pain that he'd awoken in her had shaped her features into something familiar. He suddenly found himself kissing her and felt her lips being pressed back hard onto his. He closed his eyes and inhaled her. He wanted to fall into her and be comforted by her familiarity and warmth and anise scent. The room was silent and their contact seemed to petrify them. Then he felt the warm wetness of her face and opened his eyes. Hers were still closed and for a minute Leo was looking at Laura.

He moved his face away from hers and shook his head.

Ashley opened her eyes and whispered. 'Ssssssh.' She moved her face towards him again and it was exactly like the sound Laura used to make when he had woken from a bad dream. He moved his face back towards hers but screwed his eyes tight as they touched again.

'Ssssssshhh.' Her fingers were on his cheek, the tips

touching his earlobe and sliding back to touch the skin at the nape of his neck.

Feelings that he'd forgotten suddenly surged through him and a shell felt as if it were breaking at the boundaries of his chest. In his mind he was already deep inside her, feeling her warm limbs tight about him and their mouths as one chamber. The promise of the release was excruciating. But deep down he knew that's all it would be. He was moving away from her. He broke the contact and stood looking out of the window, not seeing what was beyond it. 'I'm sorry...we can't...'

'I know...not now.' When he looked down at Ashley her eyes were still closed and her fingers were at her lips. 'How could you want me now?'

'Ash, I still love Laura.'

'But your trip to the States changed everything.'

'Bookwalter doesn't have any control over us.'

'But he does. He must have told you how legal and above board everything was.' The back of her hand streaked tears across her cheek.

'He tried to get me to sign some ludicrous piece of paperwork if that's what you mean—' Leo faltered as he took in the expression on Ashley's face and he identified the shame that had been lurking behind her anger. 'You didn't sign anything...?'

She swallowed nervously. 'I was in the middle of my divorce with nobody to turn to. I didn't know where I was going to end up.'

'You sold the photo of Laura to Bookwalter?'

Ashley neither confirmed nor denied it, tentatively waiting for his reaction.

He was suddenly aware of Ashley's tears cooling on his face.

Another tear streaked down her cheek. She knew it was pointless to speak.

Leo felt a hundred words cancel each other out and saw the wretched guilt in Ashley's expression. She looked so alone, dwarfed by the enormous sofa but Leo knew what they'd shared since Laura had left their lives was over. Ashley wasn't Laura – never could be and her confession had proved this beyond doubt. 'This is...' But nothing more came and Leo walked from the room.

Ashley didn't follow.

# CHAPTER 29

Leo became aware of his surroundings after leaving Ashley's private crescent, crossing the main road and finding himself skirting the edge of the Thames. The blurred yolk of the sun shimmered over the water but it was cold air that stole into his clothes. He realised that she'd told him what she'd done because she'd wanted to. If he'd known about her contract with Bookwalter he certainly wouldn't have kissed her. She knew this but she'd still told him anyway. He wondered if she'd always been waiting for a moment to expunge her guilt or if she'd done it because she felt she couldn't have him until she had.

His emotions were in turmoil but he was quite sure he didn't want Ashley. Not now and not before. They shared an empty space in their lives and she was a physical reminder of Laura. The two things fed off each other whenever he saw her and their relationship had grown from it.

What had happened to Laura in all this? He thought of the girl with the chipped black nails being stabbed by Bookwalter in the cemetery and the knife jutting from Coker's chest. He thought about Bonsignore being stabbed through the eye in prison and Doctor Mutatkar's body being pushed into the path of an oncoming lorry. None of it seemed to lead to her but she was steadily being consumed by it all. He could still taste Ashley's mouth on his and he thought of Laura watching them both the moment they made contact.

A woman walked past him pushing a pram and it triggered a recall of the red-haired girl in the Gristex housing complex. It felt like he had only seen her ten minutes ago and that what had happened between both their encounters had been nothing but a nightmare he'd awoken from several times on the plane.

The deep-seated nausea returned and he felt it prickling on the edge of his tongue. Days and days of ever decreasing circles had left him at the centre of the inevitable. Laura had and always would be gone and he'd never know what happened to her.

A car horn sounded but barely pierced his train of thought. He wandered down the riverbank and past the shuttered cafes and restaurants not knowing in which direction he was headed.

'Fuck off.' Cleaves responded to the horn of the car behind him, waving his arm from the open window and putting his hazard lights on. The car swerved around him and Cleaves faced forward so he couldn't see what the driver was mouthing at him as he passed. He crawled along in the car so that he could see Leo walking beside the river in his rear-view mirror and adjusted his earpiece – he'd already dialled and figured he'd waited long enough to pull Allan-Carlin out of his beauty sleep.

'Hello.' It was a very groggy female voice.

'Mr Allan-Carlin, please,' he said in as businesslike a manner as he could.

'Who the hell is this?' she croaked.

'Opallios International.' Cleaves remembered what Mr Allan-Carlin had told him to say if he ever had to call him at home.

'Just a moment...'

He heard a rustling and muted remonstration from the female voice.

'Yes?' Joe-Allan-Carlin sounded wide awake.

'He's back.'

'OK. Look, it's early here. I'll just take this call in my office.'

Cleaves waited and listened to Mrs Allan-Carlin's breathing. then there was a click and the humming atmosphere of the home office suddenly accompanied it.

'OK. Got it, Maggie – you can hang up,' Joe said sternly.

They both listened to her breathing.

'Maggie – hang it up.'

There was a slide and a clunk and her breathing was cut off.

'Where is he?' Joe didn't waste any time.

'Taking a stroll along the river.' Cleaves watched Leo pass the car and rolled another twenty yards to keep up with him.

'At this time of the morning?'

'Let's hope he doesn't do anything rash, I'd be out of a job. He's just landed, been to see his sister-in-law and now he's taking some air.' Another car beeped behind him and he waved them on.

'Stay with him and report to me when I get into the office. He hasn't been home yet then?'

'No, but I don't think he'll be calling the police.'

* * *

Leo knew that somebody had broken into the house before he discovered Mutatkar's laptop was missing. The atmosphere in the house felt different – not just the dampness of having been unoccupied – there was an alien smell when he opened the door that only briefly registered in his nostrils. Strange aftershave? It evaporated as he made his way up the hallway, but he knew that all wasn't as he'd left it.

Whoever had taken the laptop had made no attempt

to conceal their intention either. Nothing else appeared to have been taken or vandalised to give the impression of an opportunist ransacking. Leo had left the laptop on the card table in the living room. The blinds were still shut as they had been since the day he'd pored over the files. But now only the unplugged mains wire remained on the green baize.

He checked all the doors and windows but there was no sign of a break-in anywhere. This he found more unsettling than the theft. Somebody had known exactly what they wanted and taken it effortlessly without caring that he knew it.

His home had been the last place he had wanted to return to but now it was even further removed from being the shelter where he and Laura had felt safe. It was like everything he'd known had been just a wobbly bit of scenery and he was now seeing the flimsy props that held them up from behind.

He'd found nothing incriminating on the laptop but it was clear that somebody thought he might. Mutatkar had much to hide and his own answer machine message had connected him to Laura. Where else could he look for an answer from a dead man though? For all his allusiveness it was clear that Bookwalter had no connection to Mutatkar and neither did Coker. But having searched the flat in Camden he had only one option, although that already seemed exhausted.

# CHAPTER 30

'I'm not to speak to anyone.'

Leo had expected the house to be empty and had just resigned himself to the fact, when Mrs Mutatkar's voice had vibrated from the gate intercom.

He pressed the talk button. 'Mrs Mutatkar?' There was no response and Leo watched the windows of the house through the black gates. Curtains were drawn in all of them and there were no lights or movement. 'Mrs Mutatkar?' He'd been stood outside for over ten minutes and had lost count of the times he'd pressed the buzzer. 'Mrs Mutatkar, please speak to me.' Minutes passed and still there was no reply. For a moment he wondered if he'd imagined the voice but he began to speculate if she'd been told not to talk to anybody by the police – or somebody else. Her voice had sounded even more anxious than the first time he'd visited and he wondered if whoever had taken the laptop had gained access to her with similar ease.

*'I'm not to speak to anyone.'* Not 'I don't want to speak with you' or 'This is now a police matter.' Whatever the reason she was hiding, Leo guessed his first conversation with her had been his last.

\* \* \*

Leo tried to remember the last time he'd visited Matty at his King's Cross home.

He looked at his watch. It was just before 9 a.m. and he'd assumed he'd catch Matty before he went to work. There was no car in the driveway, however, and it looked as if he was going to be left on the doorstep for the second time that day. But then he heard the slam of a door within the house. He stood back a step as the oak-panelled front door opened so he could see Matty's nettled reaction to his presence through the glass porch door.

Matty looked terrible. His tight brown curls were flattened at one side of his head and he was wearing an ill-fitting indigo dressing gown that Leo assumed was Carla's. He hadn't shaved for some days and as he opened the second door a large pile of mail hissed at its bottom edge.

'This is an unexpected surprise. How come you didn't respond to any of my messages?' He was still doing that 'say something positive first' thing but he was clearly displeased at Leo's timing.

'Sorry, Matty. If this is inconvenient...'

Matty raised his one eyebrow as if it was the understatement of the century and walked back into the house leaving the two front doors open. Leo followed him inside.

''Fraid you missed the twins.'

'Carla running them to school?'

'No, I mean you've missed them...permanently.' Matty didn't look back as he said it – just headed straight into the lounge where the big flat screen was chattering morning magazine-show gibberish. He seemed to have lost something amongst the twisted duvet that had been cast half-back from the couch and was looking around distractedly.

'You sleeping down here?' Leo immediately regretted his observation.

'Just got used to it.'

Leo suddenly realised how much the house had changed. Many of the pictures and ornaments were now absent. 'What happened?'

Matty found the remote control and turned off the TV. 'Not enough, apparently.' He dropped it onto the coffee table with a clatter and it fell off the edge. 'Coffee?'

'No, I'm fine. Are you OK?' Now he felt as if he were Matty; saying all the things he was supposed to.

'I will be. Just living on the dregs at the moment.'

He gestured around him at his props – pizza boxes, empty beer and wine bottles.

'Ash told me what you said to Laura.' He hadn't thought about how he would confront Matty but suspected it was the reason he had decided to knock the door.

Matty looked blankly at Leo. It probably wasn't easy spooling back over years of living different lies but then a trace of recognition registered, which quickly switched to bemusement. 'Well, let's not talk about me and my problems all day then.'

'I just wanted you to know that I know.'

'So, that's why you've not been returning my calls.' He picked up a cigarette box from the coffee table, shook it and then worked his way through a couple of others until he found a rattle.

'Sorry if it's made me a little anti-social,' Leo said sarcastically then felt a pang of guilt. He'd been stonewalling Matty long before his lunch with Ashley.

'When Carla and I got together, I suppose it was too much to expect you to share some of my happiness for a change.' Matty sat back on the duvet and lit up.

Leo felt his neck tighten. 'And that's what you've always done for me eh, Matty?'

'It was important to me you came.' There wasn't a trace of sadness. Matty was laying a guilt trip on him.

'Yeah? Because I bet it looked good for a while. You and Carla and the twins. I could have come and seen how it all worked out so much better for you. Shame you couldn't hold it together long enough.'

'I don't fucking believe you.' Matty leant forward to flick his cigarette into the ashtray even though he didn't need to.

'I don't have Laura any more and it looks like that's exactly what you wanted.'

Matty looked up and his mortification was unnervingly genuine. 'How could you say that?'

'Try proposing marriage to her the day she was marrying me.'

Matty froze as if something had lodged itself in the cogs of his inner mechanism. Then his fingers flicked rapidly at the ashtray. 'And that's what you believe?'

'Tell me otherwise then.'

'It's true...I wanted Laura. But then I always envied what you had...it's my lot.'

'Maybe if you hadn't spent so much time trying to steal my life you would have developed one of your own. Besides, take a look at mine now.' Leo said angrily.

'Couldn't even bring yourself to acknowledge my happiness – however fleeting you knew it would be.'

'If you thought there was a time limit then it wasn't really happiness, Matty.'

'I never asked Laura to marry me. I said that one day she might change her mind and want to. Besides that was a joke I made the first day I met her. You, me, Laura and Ash – sibling foursome. You were out of earshot and, yes, that was deliberate. Ash was there though. Probably why she felt comfortable using it as part of her story after I rejected her the same evening.'

'What? You and Ash...?'

'No, never. I could see you only tolerated her. Why would I want her? I only want what you have, remember?' Matty smiled crookedly. 'Besides, she was preparing for a divorce and I didn't want to be a retaliation against her ex's affair. We ended up back at her place and she went ballistic when I wanted to leave. The only time I saw her after that was at the wedding. She blanked me the whole day. Seems we both wanted what our siblings had but only she was prepared to take me as second best. I couldn't stick around to watch you and Laura though – before or after the wedding.'

Leo had underestimated the depth of Matty's insecurity. He now saw exactly how much of an affront everything he'd done in his life had been to his younger brother. 'So Laura and I get the blame for your unhappiness—'

'More or less.' He nodded emphatically and then dragged heavily on his cigarette. 'You've never had to watch from the sidelines, Leo, there's always been a natural evolution for you. I've always known that any contentment coming my way would be even more fleeting than yours but you could have so easily been part of it. You could have made things so much easier.'

'For me or you?'

'For both of us. The day Laura disappeared could have been the start of something new for us.'

Leo closed his eyes for a moment. 'Restored the balance, you mean. Righted the injustice.'

'But it wasn't the way I thought it would be. You didn't need me because you've never needed me.'

'I didn't need you rubbing my face in your made-to-measure family, Matty. Just add contrite husband and invite recently bereaved older brother round for family dinner. So sorry I couldn't have made you feel better.'

'Bereaved? You don't know Laura's dead.'

'I do, Matty. Laura is dead and gone...' He fought to keep his emotions in check. 'She's not coming back.' Hearing himself say it out loud was excruciating enough but the fact that he was saying it to the person least likely to understand its significance, a man who wore life like a designer shirt, made the loneliness pierce him deeper than he'd ever allowed it.

But he'd been living a life of polishing and preserving and making ready for her return. Was it any different to the sort of pretence that he always accused Matty of?

# CHAPTER 31

'And you don't think I would ever be capable of understanding how that feels?' Blue smoke poured out of Matty's nostrils.

'Matty, I still don't think that I'm fully capable of understanding it.'

'And, of course, you'd have the monopoly on that. How could your younger brother ever begin to conceive of such things?'

'No, Matty – I don't think you could.'

'You haven't even asked me why Carla and Molly and Greg aren't here.'

For a moment it occurred to Leo that something terrible had happened.

'They've gone for good and I can't even begin to understand why. I've done everything I thought I was expected to do but Carla still doesn't think it's working. Her ex used to beat her up for Christ's sake but apparently I'm still no substitute.'

'I'm sorry, Matty.' But it wasn't anything he hadn't expected to hear.

'You've lost the love of your life, Leo, and you can't for the life of you begin to comprehend it. Can you not credit me with knowing how you fucking feel?'

Leo could have told Matty that Carla really wasn't the love of his life; that once he'd spent the requisite amount of time replicating a broken heart she would eventually be replaced but, at that moment in time, he knew that Matty genuinely believed it. Despite this though, Leo didn't doubt Matty's incomprehension of why life seemed to move convincingly around him but never flow through him. Perhaps he was yet to meet the human being that would change him but perhaps it wasn't such a bad thing if he didn't.

Matty crossed his legs on the duvet – it was his way of withdrawing from Leo and he'd done it since they were kids. 'Let's just suffer apart then.'

It was a vintage Matty performance and Leo would have laughed affectionately for it because it was a momentary flashback to their childhood: sitting together on the sofa at home while Leo tried to make the best of their father staggering in drunk – knowing that he would get the brunt of any random rage while Matty cried and kicked up a fuss even though not a hair on his head would be touched. 'We've both got our fair share to work through and when we're done, we'll get together over a beer and compare wounds.' It was the most facile and crass thing for Leo to say but Matty seemed to brighten at the notion that he could be part of a mourning that Leo knew hadn't even begun.

'Just don't be afraid to pick up the telephone.' Matty's mood had apparently already shifted and he stood up quickly from the sofa as Leo turned to leave.

Leo nodded a couple of times as he headed back into the hallway.

Matty tried to smooth over the awkwardness. 'Good to clear the air...get things straight.'

Leo nodded again and opened the front door, a raw wind in his face as he headed for his original destination.

* * *

As he climbed the stairs into darkness for the second time, the same middle-aged lady with a towel around her head appeared from the room at the top of the stairs and cast her eyes over him twice as if she recognised him.

'Excuse me,' he found himself saying.

As he got closer his voice seemed to have startled her and her hand missed the knob of the bathroom door.

'I just wondered if Dr Mutatkar has had any visitors recently?'

'Number 4? Never saw him to speak to. You from the bailiffs?'

'No, I'm just looking in for him and wondered if anyone has called by recently...'

Her eyes narrowed in suspicion.

Leo wanted to know if the police had found out about the room but as he avoided her gaze he looked across the darkened landing to room 4. 'You know, messages, mail.'

'Don't think he's ever had his mail delivered here.'

He turned back to her and pulled out the room key and held it up. 'Thanks, anyway.' It seemed to relax her features a little so he jangled it along the landing until he was standing in front of the door and heard her shut herself in the bathroom.

The door cracked open again and it didn't look as if anything in the room had been touched since his last visit. He wasn't back to search for something that he wouldn't find though. He was here for the same reason as Mutatkar. He didn't want to be at home, he didn't want to be at work and he didn't want to be with Matty or Ash. Had Ash concocted the whole wedding day proposal story to make sure Matty and his rejection of her wouldn't be in the way of her plans for Leo? He no longer cared.

He closed the door behind him, collapsed on the bed and lay staring at the yellow curtains in the window. The world outside it seemed vast and grey, cold and silent and its void seemed to press in against the windowpanes. Not even Bookwalter's fantasies could comfort him now.

Mutatkar was dead and gone and he thought it unlikely that the police investigation would throw up any evidence of why the doctor would know anything about Laura's whereabouts. His wife clearly had no inkling of what happened in the hours her husband had spent here or what he'd been involved in outside his work and family existence. Perhaps there was nothing more sinister than what he'd found here, perhaps the doctor had stumbled onto something that necessitated him being silenced.

Exhaustion suddenly travelled upwards from his legs and his eyes snapped firmly shut as it reached his brain. He didn't open them for another four hours. When he did somebody else was in the room.

# CHAPTER 32

He knew there was somebody there before he opened his eyes and guessed who it was from the sound of their breathing. His eyes focused on the silhouette in the window and wondered how long she'd been watching him.

'Mrs Mutatkar?'

'I wanted to lead him here.' She wore a dark overcoat and still had her handbag slung over her shoulder. She can't have been there long.

'Who?'

'The man who threatened Sabri and me.'

Leo sat up and felt light headed. 'Who is he?'

'I don't know. I really don't. Perhaps what he wants is here though. I just want him to leave us alone.' Silence hung between them and it appeared she was waiting for Leo to speak.

'I think your husband has a lot of answers that he took with him. I found his laptop here but there was nothing on it. Then it was taken from my home. I assume that whoever that was is going to remain as ignorant as us.'

'You've found nothing?' Leo discerned the desperation strangling her voice.

'Whatever it was your husband did he was careful not to leave any traces.' Leo thought about the crack pipe in the drawer but deemed it an unnecessary detail. 'And maybe that's a good thing as far as you and your daughter are concerned. Perhaps once he's satisfied you know nothing he'll leave you alone.'

'Have you any idea what a nonsense that makes of the last twenty-nine years?'

'Yes. I think I do.' Leo lay back on the bed. 'Go back to your daughter. There's nothing for either of us here.'

Mrs Mutatkar looked around the room. 'I can't even imagine Parag sitting in this room. And what was I doing all the time he was here?'

'Believing who he was. Don't torture yourself about it.'

'Easy to say.'

Leo nodded.

'If you do ever find out what happened to your wife…I don't want you to tell me.' Mrs Mutatkar left as quietly as she'd arrived.

Leo ached all over, almost as if his body had been

pinned to the bed by a huge weight that had suddenly been removed. He didn't care if someone had followed Mrs Mutatkar to Bell Terrace, didn't care if they were dangerous. He needed to sleep properly but as his eyelids closed again, the constant traffic at the end of the terrace and its reverberation kept puncturing the membrane of his unconsciousness.

He picked up Mutatkar's MP3 player from the bedside table, pushed the phones inside his ears and wondered what sort of music the good doctor enjoyed when he took his sabbaticals from reality.

He pressed play but there was nothing but hiss. Then a voice said:

'This is Doctor Parag Mutatkar. Date, December 29th 2007.'

Leo was suddenly wide awake.

It was like listening to his answerphone message. Something creaked on the recording and Leo looked across at the armchair in the window. 'This is a recorded insurance against future events.' Clearly comfortable in the chair Mutatkar continued in a lower tone. 'I will also leave a copy of this recording in a secure deposit box, details of which I have written into my will and which will only be opened upon my death. This is your recording, just so we're both crystal clear as to what will be divulged should my safety or the safety of my family be threatened.' He swallowed and Leo wondered who was being addressed and guessed that his smudgy delivery was probably due to the pipe in the drawer. 'I will also burn this commentary to several other discs for safe keeping.' Mutatkar breathed in heavily through his mouth and it sounded like he was stealing himself for what he was about to say. His voice dropped almost to a whisper. 'On the 18th December 2007, I received a telephone call at my home asking for assistance in a very sensitive matter.'

* * *

Leo stood in darkness at the front door and as the porch light came on and illuminated him his heart continued to crawl, pounding up the back of his throat. He felt curdled by what he knew, paralysed by Mutatkar's dictaphone account and the complexion it had thrown on all the times he had knocked at the same door for comfort.

The door was unlocked and opened and Maggie Allan-Carlin peered out, clasping a quilted dressing gown around her emaciated form. She looked even more sunken than when he had recently visited and still sported the bandage on her left hand.

'Leo, what are you doing here?' she grated.

He saw the usual apprehension in her expression but now he knew why she wore it so prominently, why it was eating her away.

'I *know*, Maggie.' The words weren't big enough, not when he wanted to bellow and spit them at her. The words were even and impotent and he saw only a vague glimmer of panic in her eyes.

'*Know*? What do you know?' There were footsteps behind her. 'It's Leo.' She turned to address her husband and turned back with a placid expression that was ready to invite him in. It froze though because Leo's palm was flat on the door and shoving it inward. The door caught on her toe and she yelped as he entered the hall. The door banged loudly against the wall.

'Leo, what the hell...' Joe mustered some mortification as he knotted a chocolate silk dressing gown around his pyjamas. His eyes shifted from Maggie gripping her foot and the expression fell away as soon as he saw Leo in the light of the hallway. 'What are you doing here? I thought we agreed there was nothing else for us to discuss.' But there was no potency in his reaction and its delay spoke volumes.

'Where is she?'

# Chapter 33

The Allan-Carlins froze and Leo could only hear the hammering at his temple. There was no exchanged glance, no need for one – their dread and guilt was sickeningly apparent.

'What have you been told?' Joe swallowed quickly after he'd said it as if he'd never expected to have to say the words. Although Mutatkar had no reason to lie, Leo hadn't begun to prepare himself for this truth. Now he saw it in their faces and felt dizzy with repugnance.

Joe licked at the edge of his silver moustache. It reminded Leo of Bookwalter – guileful Bookwalter whose deceptions now paled into nothingness. He shifted from foot to foot. He was attempting damage limitation but what he was trying to conceal was still too grotesque for Leo to contemplate.

Leo looked at Maggie. She had forgotten her injured foot and was leaning against the wall, her back slowly sliding down it. She'd closed her eyes and it was like somebody had put a flame to her. Her body creased and diminished as if their terrible secret was the only thing that had filled it and that now it was out she would finally shrivel to nothing. He returned his gaze to Joe.

He seemed oblivious to Maggie and was still waiting for an answer. 'Leo? What do you think you know?'

'Everything you didn't want Mutatkar to tell me.'

Something passed across Joe's eyes that left them dull, a realisation that there was no exit.

'You were having him watched as well as me. Couldn't afford to have us meet, could you?'

Joe closed his eyes and ran his hand over his patent baldness. 'Mutatkar was a hopeless addict.' He said it as if he'd rehearsed it with himself a hundred times over.

'Very convenient, seeing as you blackmailed him into helping you by threatening to expose his habit.'

Joe seemed to wince at this. 'He was my friend... once. But he was dead to everyone long before I involved him in this mess.'

'Take me to her.' But as Leo said it he realised that after months of waiting it was the last thing he wanted anyone to do.

'What did you do to Parag?' Maggie's eyes were open again and locked onto Joe.

'He was going to expose us, Maggie. I had to stop him. I couldn't allow him...not after everything we'd been through.' His irritable tone dismissed her accusation as an irrelevance.

'You were having him watched?' she slurred, whatever she'd been drinking now getting the better of her.

Leo replied. 'And me as well...although I've always thought it was the police. When Joe found out Mutatkar had tried to contact me he had him killed then had his car rolled into traffic to make it look like an accident.'

Maggie's mouth opened and choked at Joe. 'What about Dakini...and Sabri?' Her vocal cords sounded like they were rusting away.

Joe's eyelids flickered and he ran his hand over his baldness again. 'Parag had his own death wish. It was always going to end in tears for them. I had to protect us.' Again it sounded like a mantra...something that Joe had said so many times to himself that it was now flat and emotionless.

'And what did we have left to protect, Joe...the honour of our son?'

Joe was suddenly apoplectic with rage. 'We both did what we thought was right!'

'Like wringing the life from him!' She spat it back at him.

The atmosphere vibrated with her outburst and Leo felt its significance settle on all three of them.

'It was the fall that killed Louis,' Joe insisted through a clenched jaw – a defence that had clearly long been worn out. 'He tried to push me down the stairs first. You saw it, Maggie.'

'Yes, Joe – you were trying to defend yourself against a nine stone man.' Maggie looked dazed and it was like she was arguing under hypnosis.

'And that's when you decided to pick up the phone to Doctor Mutatkar.' Leo filled the silence with what he'd learnt from the dictaphone.

Joe looked at Leo as if he'd forgotten he was there. 'Louis was still alive when he arrived but Parag couldn't save him. I couldn't believe that he couldn't save him.' Exasperation glowed on his features. 'We may as well have not involved him.'

'But then he had no choice – particularly when you threatened to disclose his addiction.' Leo recalled how Joe used to circle from a distance whenever he visited. 'I always thought that you'd taken down the photos of Louis because they were too painful to bear. Of course they were – but not for the reasons I always assumed. And so here I am with the people I mourned with, thinking that Laura's disappearance and the reward money you offered was the reason your son was taken. But he died here…at your hands.'

Joe screwed his eyes shut and his breath wavered as he inhaled it through his anger.

'It was an accident!' Leo bellowed and watched them

both flinch. 'Why couldn't you have gone to the police? Do I honestly have to accept that everything I've been through was because you couldn't bring yourself to accept your son's homosexuality?'

Joe's cheeks puffed up and he exhaled a strange laugh. He opened his eyes and there was a new gleam there, a realisation that whatever the consequences were, here was an opportunity to divulge something that would only compound what Mutatkar had whispered into Leo's ears. 'I can understand Parag's horror at allowing himself to become involved in the disposal of the body. But Parag never knew the real reason I couldn't have possibly gone to the police when Louis died.'

'Joe!' The name was like a bludgeon and Maggie's tone was suddenly guttural and resonant.

Joe ignored her. 'We'd accepted Louis' lifestyle since he was seventeen. It was never a secret to us.' Joe inhaled through his nostrils and closed his eyes momentarily. 'What we didn't know was that our only flesh and blood who was still living under our roof...was a calculating psychopath.' Joe briefly allowed the silence to settle before continuing. 'Until he came home one night and told us that he'd got involved with a female prostitute and that some sex games had gone too far. At first we didn't understand what a gay man was doing with a female prostitute – until it turned out it wasn't about sex at all. He hated women and killing them fulfilled some sick fantasy.'

'No more, Joe.' But her protest was weary – resigned to accepting that too much had already been said.

'Said he'd picked her up in his car and they'd parked up before things got out of hand. We panicked. At that stage we didn't ask him what he was doing with a woman. He told us she'd threatened him at knifepoint for his money and he'd stabbed her in the struggle. He drove the body here but said he'd decided to give himself up. He had no intention of doing so but we believed him. Said we'd help him cover up. He knew we would – knew what our attitude would be. Why sacrifice his life over curiosity gone wrong with a prostitute? She was dead, he was alive; it had been a terrible accident.' Joe moved his lips around a solid bitterness. 'A German woman had just been murdered by the Vacation Killer. It was still in the news. So we sent an email like the ones they'd been talking about and I...' He swallowed. 'Then we sent the parcel to the police...like the Vacation Killer had been doing. It seemed like the perfect opportunity to misdirect.'

'Louis murdered Teresa Strickland?'

'We only realised it hadn't been an accident when Vicky Cordingley died. He kept their underwear as trophies. Maggie found them in his room. He knifed Cordingley in the same way. Our son liked hurting girls. And he knew we'd still have to help him.'

'I wanted to go to the police,' Maggie said to the wall opposite her.

'And what would have been the point in that?' Joe snapped. 'We were all implicated. We had to do exactly what we did before.'

'Like clockwork.' Her words were dried thin.

'Louis told us it was going to stop but I knew it wouldn't. We argued...we fought...and he fell down the stairs. That's when I first telephoned Parag. He couldn't save him though. Louis had broken his spine.'

'You pushed him,' Maggie accused.

Joe's eyes shifted to Maggie and then back again without a glimmer. 'So we had to cover up in the same way – using the Vacation Killer. But Laura came into the office and saw the email about Louis before it was sent.'

'What did you do to her?' Leo visualised himself sitting in Chevalier's.

'It was the last thing we expected to happen but she walked back in at the wrong time.' There was pleading in Joe's voice.

'What did you do to her, Joe? Enough to justify the reward money you offered?'

But it was Maggie who answered. 'She said she was out Christmas shopping for the afternoon. I composed the email from the Vacation Killer after she'd left. Joe had set up an untraceable email facility that we could access from anywhere. I shouldn't have done it from work but we were short on time and I thought the office was empty. I had to make an urgent visit to the ladies;

301

when I came back Laura was standing in front of the monitor reading it. She had her scarf in her hand, the one she'd forgotten. I'd seen it on the back of her chair... should have thought she might come back for it. She was still clasping it when we got her back here. I could have told her that the email had been sent to me. Could easily have bluffed it...'

'Yes...' Joe hissed.

'I panicked. I hit her with the Krug bottle...the one everyone put their pennies into. She'd only just emptied it and was going to use the money to buy drinks for the Christmas party. I hit her with it once and then Joe carried her down to our car and drove her back here.'

'Drove her back here and locked her in the air raid shelter.' Leo used Parag Mutatkar's account that was still fresh in his ears. 'Locked her in there but couldn't decide what to do with her.'

'She fell ill a few days later.' Maggie tried to swallow a chunk of the memory. 'We couldn't open the door but I slipped notes under it – asking her what she needed.'

'Did you really believe you could keep her locked in there for ever?'

Maggie didn't shift her focus from the wall. 'So Joe called Parag again. We knew he wouldn't go to the police. He sedated her while she was asleep and examined her. She had hypoglycemia. She wasn't eating any of the food we were leaving for her inside the entrance door. He told us he could treat her. Give her injections while she was asleep.'

Leo felt a mass expanding in his chest. 'But he couldn't treat her, could he? And while you were making your minds up what to do with her Parag failed you again...'

But neither Joe nor Maggie were looking at him. They were both suddenly looking up at the doorway behind Leo. The hallway was suddenly bathed in light, like a flash capturing the expressions in front of him. He heard the crunch afterwards and realised it was something impacting his skull before he hit the floor unconscious.

# CHAPTER 34

'How's my timing?'

Cleaves squeezed his knuckles. They were going to balloon but he knew they weren't broken. In the absence of a makeshift cosh he'd known the force that had been necessary to apply at the base of Leo's skull.

Maggie was rooted to the spot in shock but Joe moved to the bottom of the stairs to sit down.

Cleaves was shaking his throbbing hand like a thermometer. 'What do you want to do here?'

Joe rubbed his face and then clasped a hand over his baldness.

'Looks like things are racking up for the pair of you.' Cleaves continued.

Joe lifted his head. He clearly didn't like the

cheerfulness in Cleaves' tone. 'It seems I'll be extending our contract.'

Cleaves nodded and moved so he was standing with his feet either side of Leo's waist. 'Where shall I put this?' He hoped disposing of Sharpe was going to be more straightforward than Mutatkar.

* * *

Leo knew he was somewhere dark before he opened his eyes. It was pitch black but he knew it wasn't blindness. The bruise at the back of his skull began to hammer louder than the circulation in his ear and his eyes refused to adjust or find any shades within the solidity around him. His spine ached and it felt like he'd fallen down a flight of stairs. He felt the backs of his hands against his lips and moved them slowly apart expecting his wrists to be bound. They weren't but they immediately struck something solid and cool in front of them.

He ran his fingers over the area and heard his suddenly animated breath bouncing back from it. He slid his palms above his head and back down again and found the same flat surface. He heard himself grunt in panic and started to push against it. His body slid back as he pushed and then it felt as if he was suspended in mid air. A second later he fell and his spine jarred with a harsh impact.

Disoriented he lay still for a few moments, feeling the invigorated pain shriek at the top of his spine.

The acoustics of his position seem to change and his irregular breaths no longer fell back on his face. There was a free flow of cooler air about him and he lifted his right hand. His knuckles butted painfully against something and he cried out. But whatever it was had an edge and he curled his fingers around it. It was a long metallic bar and above it was something soft. He felt over it and rested his fingertips on the cool, sprung surface there.

He took a few breaths and let his veins decelerate. He'd fallen from a bed and was now lying on his back on the floor below it. He calculated he must have woken on his side and pushed himself away from the wall. It was small comfort though because he still couldn't see anything and didn't know where he was – although he already guessed where he could be.

He rolled painfully away from the edge of the bed and onto his side. Every muscle ached awkwardly like they'd been removed and stuffed back into place. He teetered on the side of his ribs and then tipped onto his front pulling his legs in so his knees could take some of the weight.

He breathed in the cool concrete floor and didn't doubt that he was in the air raid shelter at the bottom of Maggie and Joe's land. It was the place they'd incarcerated Laura, the place she had spent her last days before Parag had failed to save her. This is where she'd been while he'd sat at home and at the police station and patrolled the streets around the Opallios offices.

He was surprised to still find himself alive. Did they not have the guts to dispose of him or were they just going to leave him in here to expire in his own time? He bowed his head and started to crawl on his hands and knees anticipating his head butting into a wall or a door. The room was bound to be small but he wanted to get an idea of the layout

*Let me out of here!* His brain shrieked it first and he drew breath as he prepared to retch the words from his lungs. But as he inhaled he detected a smell.

Suddenly he felt another impact on the back of his head – he'd been hit again though not half as hard as before. What was the smell though? In his unbalanced state it took him a few moments to successfully identify it. His head throbbed but it didn't seem to matter because he'd identified the scent.

'*Laura?*'

Leo wondered if he'd been drugged and if his senses were playing cruel tricks on him but as he tried to focus on his surroundings through the cacophony of pain in his head he detected a movement to his left. It was a soft almost indiscernible drag sound like somebody pulling their feet into themselves.

'Laura,' he said louder and held his breath. Blood coursed around his brain but he kept his lungs locked tight until he was positive he could hear somebody else drawing air from the same direction. He screwed his eyes tight. 'Please don't hit me again. I'm not here to harm you.' It wafted over him now, Laura's breath, Laura's scent.

'Leo.' The word was like a bubble, bursting wet and unformed from the back of her throat.

For a moment the pain ceased, as if something had pinched its artery and momentarily halted the flow. Leo didn't move, didn't open his eyes, but felt heat building behind his face. Then he crawled in the direction of the word. The first thing his finger touched was Laura's foot. His fingers curled around the warmth through her sock and scrabbled upwards, connecting with the solid edge of her knee and clumsily striking her breast as it moved higher. His body shifted around the space she occupied and he felt a palm on his shoulder. Then his face touched the coolness of her neck, squeezing tightly against a part of it as his fingers sought her. Her nose pressed into the side of his eye and he felt her hair tangling in his fingers as he sought the back of her head.

Their bodies compacted and neither of them breathed as their arms pulled themselves harder against each other and he felt his bottom lips brush the top of her ear. They didn't speak, just gripped themselves to each other, shoulders spasming, eyes swelling and all Leo could think of was what Maggie had said when she'd told him she'd been to see her medium.

*'She's in a comfortable place now.'*

His brain accelerated in hundreds of directions: Laura, Maggie, Joe, Mutatkar, Louis. Leo couldn't believe how immediate the truth had always been, how close by Laura had waited as they'd watched events he had no connection to unfold on the TV in the Allan-Carlin's lounge. He recalled the view through their double-glazing extending to the place she had been a prisoner since the day she'd walked back to the Opallios offices to pick up her scarf. Joe and Maggie would have had plenty of time to replace the footage from their own security cameras so it looked like Laura had never gone back.

'Where are we?' she whispered.

Hearing her voice, the voice that he never thought he'd hear again brought the needles back to his shoulders the way they'd prickled when he'd walked back into Chevalier's when he knew she'd vanished. Mutatkar had said she'd died, that he hadn't been able to administer the correct medication in time. At no point had he ever said he'd been involved in her disposal though – like he had Louis. The Allan-Carlins must have told him she was dead in order to guarantee his silence.

If Mutatkar had been as guilt ridden as he'd sounded in the Dictaphone recording, then it was possible he would have eventually talked. His message on the answering machine proved this. Perhaps the news about Bonsignore's death had prompted him to at last reveal what had happened, having believed Laura was dead and that it had been his fault. 'We're getting out of here.' He felt the rawness of his emotion haemorrhage in his throat.

'How did you find me?' Her head pressed itself into the crook of his throat and he smelt shampoo.

'Mutatkar said you were dead. Maggie and Joe must have lied to him.'

'Maggie and Joe?'

Their names hung in the air and Leo knew what her response meant. 'They've been holding you here.' His arms were round her slight frame but it didn't feel as if she had been starved.

'Maggie and Joe.' She repeated their names as if the words were alien to her.

'Do you remember seeing an email Maggie composed?'

'I remember going back to Opallios...picking up my scarf and then waking here.'

Perhaps Laura's memory of what had been on the screen had been wiped clean by Maggie's blow with the bottle but Leo felt the beginnings of a grim realisation. Had she been imprisoned for all this time on the basis of a single misconception? They thought she had seen the email and so could never free her because Laura would not only implicate them but lead police to the dark secret that they'd been hiding. He felt his own hostility begin to expand inside him – pushing the pain and its sounds to the edge.

'What email?' He felt her body tauten.

'Louis Allan-Carlin was a murderer. Maggie was trying to cover for him and she thought you knew.'

'But they were the ones who offered a reward. I saw it on my TV down here.'

'A reward they knew nobody was going to claim.'

Laura was sitting up now, stretching her limbs when Leo just wanted to hold onto her.

'Has there never been any light in here?' He wanted to distract her now, not overload her with a truth that she couldn't even start to absorb.

'They only turn off the lights when they're bringing things into the shelter. I nearly escaped a couple of weeks ago. Think I broke someone's fingers when I shut them in the door.'

Leo recalled the bandage on Maggie's hand.

'Did they hurt you?'

'I've never seen them...now I understand why.' She inhaled heavily. 'I think they drug my food. Often I wake up and find they've been in. *Maggie and Joe...*' Laura was obviously having difficulty pasting their faces onto those of her captors. 'I thought you were one of them. The lights were turned off and somebody held me down, put a swab on my face. Somebody big.'

Leo wondered if it was the same person who had struck him on the back of his head and if it was the man who had nearly collided with his car when he left the Allan-Carlins the last time. He'd always thought the police had been following him but it looked like Joe had had both Leo and Mutatkar monitored in case they ever got close to the truth. The watcher was obviously the man who had stolen the laptop and had been threatening Mrs Mutatkar.

'When I woke up I knew I wasn't alone.'

He felt her breath against his skin when she spoke and its sensation vied with all the other emotions surging through him. 'Laura, how long have I been here?'

'I've been awake for about half an hour. I don't know how long you were here before then.'

Conversing with her seemed dreamlike and he wondered if he was about to wake at his security desk as he had so many times in the past. Then suddenly the harsh lights came on and he had to shut his eyes to the brightness.

# CHAPTER 35

Somebody was rattling the door handle but the light was too intense. He heard slow metallic clunks to his left but he kept his screwed up eyes to Laura, feeling her body against his fingertips as he suddenly clung to her frame, petrified she might evaporate.

But as he stretched his eyelids apart again, details started to soak through the bleached backdrop and the first thing he noticed was how long her hair was. She hadn't worn it that length since she was in school but her henna hair lay well past her shoulders down her back. He studied her intensely as her pale features acquired detail. Suddenly he felt a part of himself ignite, a whole network of feeling that he'd forgotten was there.

Her dirt-streaked tears blurred as his own eyes filled and he doubted he could move them from her to find out who was grating at the entrance to the shelter. Her skin was paler, her features more gaunt, but she was Laura. Laura was alive. Laura was OK. His mind recoiled against these thoughts – a reflex that had honed itself over the months she had been locked here – but her presence, the weight of her, her freckled eyes narrowing to see him was irrefutable.

Her eyes darted from his and he followed their direction. He briefly took in the place where Laura had spent her imprisonment. They appeared to be crouching in the main living area, which was about ten foot square. To his right was another doorway to a small cubicle where a green porcelain toilet and small sink accounted for most of the space within. Around the concrete floor of the living room were scattered blankets, a food tray, clothes, magazines and newspapers and Leo was surprised to see a TV and cable box positioned on top of a small bookcase. The whitewashed walls were lined with shelves and their cluttered contents – from tubes of cosmetics to tins of food – precariously bowed the cheap Formica.

But he had no time to absorb everything as they heard locks being shot at the other side of the heavy, metallic, inner door that had separated them for so long.

Leo was on his feet, pulling Laura up with him. As he thought of her waiting, breathing, existing in this place while he had searched and given up hope, he felt a concentration within him, a snap distillation of the rage that had been awaiting its release.

The door was released from its frame, and as the weight eventually gave it impetus, it slowly started to swing inwards. A cold draught blew into the shelter but neither of them shivered. Leo could smell the night before the door opened fully, revealing the solid blackness of space outside. Nobody entered but neither of them made a move. Leo's eyes fully readjusted and he could discern the other door that had been opened into the small antechamber that led into the shelter. Somebody moved in the darkness outside but the shaded lamp above smudged their view beyond the doorframe. Whoever was out there could see them perfectly though and suddenly Leo felt their exposure.

But whatever awaited them outside was better than the prospect of being locked in again. Leo led Laura by the hand to the doorway to hide at its edge and peer round. Through a small copse he could see glimpses of the yellow lights in the house windows but there was no light source to illuminate the dark expanse in front of them. There was nobody in evidence but whoever had opened the door had to be nearby. They listened and a fox cried off somewhere nearby but there was no sounds of human movement.

Then a face materialised slowly from the black, the light spilling from the shelter highlighting their skin as their body composed itself beneath it. It was Maggie.

Weakly, she held up her hand to placate Leo as he moved into the doorway.

'Come quickly,' she rasped and Leo noticed a blob of thick, blackening blood on her eyebrow. She stared past him as Laura emerged behind him. It was the first time Laura had seen her captor and Maggie seemed terrified of revealing herself. 'It's all gone wrong. Leo, you have to help me.'

Leo felt Laura unlacing her fingers from his, breaking away from him and moving forward but he suddenly grabbed her wrist and yanked her back. 'Wait, this is a trap!'

Maggie shook her head in Leo's foreground but his eyes scanned the area behind her. Where was Joe? And what about the man who had struck him from behind? Silhouetted by the light from the shelter they were sitting targets.

'No, no, no,' Maggie whispered, her breath escaping her in a cloud before she staggered and fell to one knee in the long wet grass. She put her hand to her brow, staining her fingertips. Her eyes rolled and it looked like she was concussed. 'I begged Joe not to kill Laura.' A fat tear dropped onto the grass. 'It was me that prevented him. Help me now, Leo.'

Laura yanked herself from Leo's grip and stood over her. Maggie didn't raise her head just stared at Laura's jeans.

'Forgive me, Laura. Understand. I kept you alive...'

Leo watched Laura's shoulders quake and the tremor travel down her body as she balled her fingers into fists.

'Laura, there's no time...' He walked to where she stood and put his hands on her rigid shoulders. 'Come on.' He tried to move her but it was as if she had been pegged into the grass.

'Poison...' Maggie had started to shiver, her bottom jaw vibrating around the word.

'What are you talking about?' Leo moved from behind Laura and knelt with Maggie as he tried to hear what she said.

'We tried to poison Cleaves but he won't die. He's gone mad. He's going to kill Joe. Please stop him.'

'What are you talking about?' He gripped her shoulders now and shook her until her she faced him.

'He knows everything. He's another liability. I put the poison in his brandy.'

'What sort of poison?'

'The poison we...Joe wanted us to use it a long time ago.' Maggie looked briefly up at Laura and then her body collapsed forward and she was face down in the grass.

# CHAPTER 36

Leo was suddenly engulfed in darkness again, the lights from the house the only beacon. He circled his hand firmly around Laura's wrist and led the way along the well-trodden path towards the main house. The only thing in his head was the sound of his own breathing and one thought: Joe Allan-Carlin could not die yet. Joe Allan-Carlin was going to suffer like Laura had. Cleaves – whoever he was – wasn't going to end it easily for him.

Branches bit his face and eyes as they entered the thickest part of the copse but soon they were emerging into the lawn and pool area. Laura gulped air as they halted between the twin pillars of light being cast by the double-glazing.

'Wait here. If I'm not back in a couple of minutes—'

Laura coughed and shook her head violently. It was pointless arguing and Leo was reluctant to ever let her out of his sight again. They walked slowly to the house and stepped through the window that was slid back. They were inside the coral-carpeted lounge where he had sat and watched the irrelevant news reports with Joe and Maggie over the years – the Vacation Killer, the release of Bookwalter, Bonsignore – and the only thing he could feel was revulsion for his own stupidity.

Silence. The familiar surroundings seemingly the most unlikely backdrop for what had been concealed here. The room was unoccupied. Leo looked round for a weapon but there was nothing that could be brandished. He pulled Laura to the door that led into the kitchen. The door swung inward revealing chunks of glass lying shattered on the tiles. Nobody was there either. Leo's shoes ground against the shards as he headed for the magnetic knife rack on the wall over the cooker.

A muffled bump from upstairs only momentarily stopped him in his tracks. He turned to face Laura and the direction of the sound. Laura turned to the door into the hallway but there was no fear in her expression. He looked at her slender body clad in a stonewashed blue sweatshirt that he recalled Joe wearing on one of his visits. At the end of her jeans her white-socked feet stood in the glass and a trail of blood was already smeared behind her.

Leo nodded downwards but Laura didn't follow his

gaze – merely nodded. Leo snatched a Chinese cleaver from the rack and led Laura limping over the tiles, through the swing door into the hall so they were standing at the bottom of the carpeted stairwell.

There was another thump and a voice he didn't recognise grunted a curse. The front door was before them and Leo knew their best course of action would be to unlock it and run, but neither of them made a move towards it. Their gaze was trained on the stairwell and Leo's knuckles whitened around the handle of the cleaver. He remembered how Coker had held his knife before he'd tried to kill him. It was like it had been slotted into that moment – his murderous intent lodging it there. This was how the blade felt, like it had no other purpose.

Leo tried to release Laura's hand but her fingertips bit into his wrist and she followed him as he steadily climbed the stairs. As they rounded the corner of the first flight and ascended the second to the landing, there was another thump and then a splitting sound.

Leo peered down the illuminated landing and saw Cleaves against the door at the far end. He turned and looked at Leo but didn't seem bothered by his presence or the blade Leo was carrying. Cleaves stretched his neck away from his body and the tendons straining there seemed to be barely holding his shaved head on his shoulders. His nostrils flared and he inhaled through them erratically. He slammed his huge body against the door but the effort was too much for him and he slid to his knees as he rebounded from it. He ground his forehead into the wood and gritted his teeth against an internal spasm that tangled his gut. 'What...the fuck...did you give me?' Although his voice was resonant, it seemed he was having trouble putting the words together. He stood shakily before thrusting his shoulder back against the door again. Another crack but Leo wasn't sure if it was the door or the bones in his shoulder.

Cleaves slid down the door again but this time he was on his knees and burying his face in the carpet as a convulsion squeezed a howl from somewhere deep within him. His grey suit jacket had flapped over his head and he looked like some headless animal in its death throes.

Leo felt Laura's hand on his shoulder as he attempted to move forward and she tried to yank him back.

Cleaves was not yet beaten and got to his feet again. Leaning against the wall opposite the door, he aimed his boot at the handle but was suddenly overwhelmed by another paroxysm of pain in his gut. He braced himself against the spasm and tried to aim straight. The kick made the door rattle within the frame and it sounded as if metallic pieces of the lock mechanism were fragmenting as he repeatedly booted the handle. He grunted with each impact but as his impetus slowed he slammed his head back against the wall and opened his mouth. Suddenly, his body seized up and his eyes closed against the pain. His whole weight collapsed against the door, his head taking the entire impact and grazing itself open on the splintered wood, before coming to rest on the carpet. And then he was still.

Whatever he'd been dosed with had acted rapidly even on his considerable build and it didn't bear thinking about how Laura would have suffered if Joe had got his way. They both watched as Cleaves' chest stopped heaving.

Now it was Leo's shoulder on the door, Leo rattling the broken handle and trying to gain entry and he didn't care if he had to shatter every bone to open it. In his mind all his adversaries cowered on the other side – Joe, Maggie, Bookwalter, Coker – and now he knew them Leo no longer doubted he was as capable of destroying their lives as they had been destroying his. The blade was part of his hand now, his intent fusing it there until its only purpose had been fulfilled.

Cleaves had done considerable damage to the door already and a renewed assault caused the top-right corner to crack and hinge inward. He butted himself against the lower part, his wrist and shoulder crushing against the wood and the flat of the blade. Soon the rest of the lock side split and he was able to kick in the bottom part until it was clear of the lock and the whole thing swung inward.

The first thing he saw was Joe's face. The knife

handle was firm in Leo's throbbing fingers and he heard Laura scream from somewhere behind him. Suddenly Joe rushed at him, grunted and then moved away again, his reddened features recoiling in shock as he stepped back and tripped over the desk behind him. Pens, ornaments, other things on the study table rattled to the floor.

Then they both looked down at the brass handle of the letter opener that Joe Allan-Carlin had stabbed into Leo's chest. Joe slid slowly down the wall, his eyes screwing tight against what he'd done. He placed his hands over the back of his head in resignation as Leo collapsed and lay listening to Joe's sobs. Then everything started to fade, and Leo could hear no more.

# EPILOGUE

On the night of March 3rd, 2009, police were summoned to the household of Joe and Maggie Allan-Carlin. The couple were arrested and later charged with the murder of Anthony Cleaves.

They are currently assisting the police re the murders of Teresa Strickland, Vicky Cordingley, Louis Allan-Carlin, Doctor Parag Mutatkar and the kidnap of Laura Sharpe.

After hospitalisation, Leo Sharpe made a full recovery and returned home with his wife.

Following police interviews with Leo Sharpe, a warrant was issued for the arrest of Wesley Coker. Coker had recently received medical attention at his home after surviving injuries sustained from an intruder but had made almost a full recovery. Jud Samuel, Petroleum County Sheriff, was shocked at what they discovered when he led FBI agents to Coker's home on the Gristex complex. Coker had been murdered and dismembered – his limbs arranged like a clock face.

John R Bookwalter had already been arrested on suspicion of murdering a prostitute. It became apparent that prior to this arrest he'd overcome his reluctance to leave the state of Louisiana and he immediately confessed to Coker's murder. His name glowed brightly for a few weeks as Howard Bonsignore's confession was recanted. Bookwalter is now awaiting trial.

It was Wesley Coker, however, who was immediately accorded his place in criminal history as the genuine Vacation Killer.

© theykillagain.com

# ACKNOWLEDGEMENTS

Thanks to you for picking up this book, to Ben Mason at Conville and Walsh for faith and incisive input, Lara Crisp at Allison & Busby for conviction and enthusiasm and Madame Butterfly and Flying Officer Kite for giving me everlasting love.